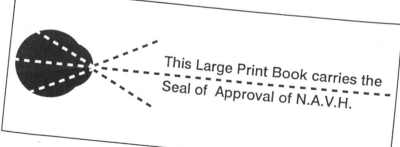

Curtain For A Jester

A Mr. and Mrs. North Mystery

Frances and Richard Lockridge

Thorndike Press • Thorndike, Maine

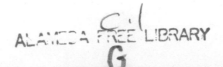

Library of Congress Cataloging in Publication Data:

Lockridge, Frances Louise Davis.
   Curtain for a jester : a Mr. and Mrs. North mystery
/ by Frances and Richard Lockridge.
      p.   cm.
   ISBN 1-56054-238-1 (alk. paper : lg. print)
   1. Large type books. I. Lockridge, Richard, 1898-
II. Title.
[PS3523.O243C87   1992]   91-41347
813'.54—dc20   CIP

Thorndike Press Large Print edition published in 1992
by arrangement with HarperCollins Publishers.

Large Print edition available in the British
Commonwealth by arrangement with Curtis Brown, Ltd.

Cover design by Harry Swanson.

The tree indicium is a trademark of Thorndike Press.

This book is printed on acid-free, high opacity paper.

CURTAIN FOR A JESTER

I

Wednesday, April 1: 8:45 P.M.
to 11:46 P.M.

Pamela North came from her bathroom and said, "Rubber spiders." For a moment, Gerald North continued to look, with reproach, at the reflection of a black bow tie. He sighed; he pulled a tie end, prepared to start over. He said, "At least rubber spiders," and Pam moved so that she too was reflected in her husband's mirror. Jerry turned with pleasure, regarded her and said he could see she was all ready for the party. "I am, really," Pam said. "Everything that takes time's done. Putting on clothes is nothing."

She sat on an ottoman in front of her dressing table and began to put on stockings. "Snakes, too, with springs in them," Pamela North said, clipped the stockings to a garter belt, put on spike-heeled slippers and, teetering on first one foot and then the other, stepped into white silk pants. "You've got to start with the ends even," she said. Jerry, who had started with the ends even, said, "Umm-m," looped, pulled through and straightened. "You're sure Mr. Wilmot was the one

7

about the windowpanes?" Pam said, and put on a bra. "I remember it as somebody else."

"Somebody helped him, of course," Jerry said. He decided the bow would do, and turned from the mirror. "Even with two, it must have taken most of the night."

"The trouble people will go to," Pam said, from under her dress. She came out the top of the dress. "Just to embarrass people. Turning mirrors inside out."

It had not, Jerry told her, been done with mirrors, although Wilmot had been, in his day, quite a man with mirrors. It had been done with special window glass — panes of glass through which one could look without being looked at, from one side normally transparent, from the other opaque. Wilmot and his associate, working at night — after bribing a watchman — had reversed three such panes in the steel frames waiting to be installed in a building under construction. The building was a dormitory at a New England college for women. The windows had been planned for, and were duly placed in, a communal shower room on the first floor. It had been some days — some sidewalk-crowded days — before the prank was discovered.

"Still a lot of trouble," Pam said. "And what have you got? Zip."

Jerry moved to his wife's back. He zipped.

8

He found the two tiny hooks, the incredibly fragile loops of thread, and joined two and two, feeling his fingers monstrous. "A joke," he said. He kissed the back of Pam's neck, lightly. He said, "Zipped," and was thanked. "Of course," he said, "they were both young then. Wilmot and whoever it was."

"It's not enough," Pam said, and moved to look at herself in the mirror in the door. She turned from side to side, looked over the left shoulder, over the right. "You still like it?" she asked. Jerry nodded. "They do go to more trouble when there's a man along," Pam said. "Although Miss Shapiro is wonderful even if there isn't." She faced the mirror again. "It doesn't too much?" she asked. "I mean, I'm not on television." She was told it was fine.

"I do keep thinking of rubber spiders," Pam North said. "I like you in a dinner jacket. Your tie's a little crooked, though. Right ear, just a touch." Jerry straightened the tie, while Pam sat at the dressing table, twisting bright hair into final arrangement. She said, "Umm-m-m" and, with tissue, adjusted lipstick. "I still don't see why he invited us," she said, and turned her back on the mirror. "Don't really see. Or quite why we're going."

"Because he's long wanted to meet us, and I quote," Gerald North said. "Because it's the sort of party that we, especially, might find interesting. Because you want to wear the new dress."

"Why we especially?" Pam said, not denying the new dress. "Do you suppose, authors?"

She made them, Jerry told her, sound a little like rubber spiders. She might be right, of course. It was conceivable that Mr. Byron Wilmot, tenant for some months of the penthouse which topped the apartment building in which the Norths also lived, thought that party association with authors might be especially interesting to a publisher. Or, obscurely, Mr. Wilmot might be having one of his little jokes — his famous little jokes. They had, Jerry mentioned, been over it already.

To that Pamela North agreed, although noting that going over it was one thing. They had been going over it, at intervals, since Mr. Wilmot's polite note of invitation had arrived three days before. A party to be given, honoring All Fools, on the night of the Day of All Fools. And Mr. Wilmot thought that the Norths, of whom he had heard so much, might find it the kind of party in which they would be especially interested. Before they accepted, and afterward, they had still gone over it. It was conceivable that Mrs. North's new dress had been the deciding point. But curiosity had undeniably entered in.

They had seen Mr. Wilmot only once, and then had merely smiled in the vague manner of tenant meeting tenant in an elevator. The Norths had been in the elevator — which Pam considered semi-automatic, since it had an operator by day — except when tenants called him to other duties — and was tenant-manipulated by night — and a plump man, who was about to become a fat man, entered. He beamed impartially; the operator said, "Good evening, Mr. Wilmot." The Norths smiled noncommittal smiles. This association continued to the fourth floor, where the Norths seeped around Mr. Wilmot, who obligingly pulled himself in, or made motions of doing so. The elevator then bore Mr. Wilmot to more remote, and expensive, heights.

"So that's Wilmot," Gerald North had said, putting key in lock. "Wonder if he's ever thought of writing a book?"

As a publisher, Gerald North was interested in people who might consider writing books. They at once attracted and repelled him.

"Why?" Pam asked, when they were in their apartment, when she was crouched on the floor, surrounded by Siamese cats who had been left too long, and wished to talk clamorously of a lonely afternoon. "Th'

11

Teeney, th' Gin, th' Sherry. Th' *babies!* What about? *Teeney!* Leave her *alone!*" (The cat Martini hissed moderately and slapped her blue-point daughter on the right ear, for impenetrable reasons of her own. Sherry drew back, remained bland.)

"If it's the right Wilmot," Jerry had said, "and I did hear some place he'd moved in here, he's a legend. Byron Wilmot. The life of the party. Remember?"

Pam remained among the cats, but looked up. It came to her, then. She said, "*That* Wilmot." She considered. "You mean," she said, "he's still alive?"

He appeared to be, Jerry told her. Alive, and in good flesh. He granted that it was as if a myth walked.

"Because," Pam said, "it's all so — I don't know — twentyish? Was he the ditch across Fifth Avenue?"

Jerry thought he was not, but that he must have envied those gay spirits who, in the gayer past, had procured barricades and "Men Working" signs and suitable clothes and tools, and had dug a trench at least part way across upper Fifth Avenue, while a cooperative policeman diverted traffic around them. Wilmot had been, no doubt as he grew older and less inclined to jokes so physically strenuous, one of the busiest employers of comic waiters, famous spillers of soups, quarrelers with guests. It was Wilmot, notoriously, who had briefly transformed a bootblack of his acquaintance into an Italian nobleman; he who, with an accomplice and a life-sized doll, had so realistically simulated baby snatching that, in the ensuing turmoil, his accomplice had been slightly shot.

Since a certain tolerance surrounds the practical joker — a tolerance most evident, of course, in those not butts of his jests — Byron Wilmot had achieved that affectionate, if wary, regard commonly bestowed on large puppies. He was, it was widely considered, always good for a laugh. What *that* Wilmot would be up to next was beyond anticipation. (That it was also very nearly beyond tolerance was the conviction of only the dourest of spoilsports.) It was by many considered the cream of the jest that Byron Wilmot had not only had his little jokes, but in the end had made them pay. Beginning in his college days as the purest of amateurs, he had subsequently turned professional. Mr. Wilmot, increasingly jovial as he grew older (and increasingly rotund), became also "The Novelty Emporium." The motto of the Novelty Emporium was "Anything For A Laugh."

And for those who laughed at boutonnieres provided with cold running water, explosive cigars — Mr. Wilmot did not hold himself superior to the obvious — highball glasses which leaked, and others which, on being touched, subsided disconsolately into wrinkled monstrosities, toilet-paper holders which played tunes as they turned, simulated ink spots, fountain pens which spit back, hideously lifelike tarantulas of rubber and snakes which writhingly propelled themselves, daggers with retracting blades and bladders of a fluid which uncomfortably resembled blood, toy pistols designed to frighten the innocent, toilet seats contrived to embarrass the modest — for such devotees of the authentic bellylaugh, the Novelty Emporium did provide everything. Amateur magicians could find there numberless devices of illusion. Those who fancied alarming facial masks could make of themselves monsters to terrify the young, and costumes of repulsive grotesqueness were available for purchase, or might be rented.

Not a few of the more ingenious of such novelties, Mr. Wilmot had himself designed. Some of them, as a subsidiary of himself, he manufactured. As he flourished, not an inventor of realistic glass eyes (to be found by someone in a bowl of soup) or of artificial scars (to be affixed when the purpose was to revolt) but went first to Mr. Wilmot, confident of backing. Salesmen of horrendous

14

puppets beat a path to his door.

Among his objects of trade, Mr. Wilmot himself was often to be found, and when he was found he beamed. Displaying collapsible cutlery to favored customers, Mr. Wilmot would shake with laughter; one was left feeling that he could hardly bring himself to barter away objects of such infinite delight. (His predicament a little, some could not help thinking, resembled that of Omar Khayyám's vintners.) But Mr. Wilmot could be brought to sell and his staff — which had grown considerably by the 1950's — sold with alacrity. Business was only slightly seasonal — the days before April first were, of course, the best, but the Novelty Emporium did well, also, before Christmas. Toys were heavily stocked at the latter period, and not all of them were designed to throw children into convulsions.

In short, Mr. Wilmot prospered, the roundest of pegs in a perfectly rounded hole. He had, in the truest sense, made jokes practical. " 'Laugh, and the world laughs with you,' " Mr. Wilmot said now and again, when in a philosophic mood. For the privilege, a sufficient part of the world was willing to pay. So Mr. Wilmot ran to penthouses. He ran to penthouse parties.

Pamela North tried a necklace and discarded

it, and tried another. Jerry, at the last moment, retied his tie and Pam, ready, said only, "See, darling?" They went from the bedroom and it was late. In the living room the cats arose from resting places and preceded the Norths to the door. The Norths, Pam first, slid through the smallest of negotiable openings, and Jerry warded cats away with a foot. The seal points swore; Sherry assured the world that her heart was broken. The Norths crossed to the elevator.

Party or no party, the elevator became fully automatic after nine. Jerry pressed the button; the elevator gave off sounds of its approach. It stopped and the door opened and a tall, dark man, with a neatly trimmed mustache, started to get out. He stopped, however, almost at once and said, "Not the penthouse, is it? I must have — "

"I'll be damned," Jerry North said. "Art Monteath. I thought you were in London. Or somewhere."

Arthur Monteath would be as damned as Jerry, as Pamela might be supposed to be. They were the last people he could imagine running into, there of all places.

"But Mr. Monteath," Pam said. "We live here. We — "

The elevator door attempted to close itself, having waited its appointed time. The Norths stepped in, as Monteath stepped back.

"You're not going to this do of Wilmot's?" Monteath said.

"But we are," Pam said. "In spite of rubber spiders."

The elevator, as if shrugging off this nonsense, started up. It had the twelfth floor to reach; instructions had been given.

"I was going to get in touch with you," Monteath told Jerry North.

"A book?" Jerry said. There was something in his voice, and Monteath laughed.

"Don't let it scare you," Monteath said. "Not mine. The old man's. The ambassador's. I'll give you a ring about it. I didn't realize you knew Wilmot."

The elevator stopped, sighed, and opened its door. They emerged in the twelfth floor corridor.

"We still have to climb a flight," Pam said, and held her skirt a little from the floor, and walked toward the flight to be climbed. Monteath and Jerry walked with her. "We don't really know Mr. Wilmot," Pam said. "Except in the elevator, of course. I suppose you — ?"

"Haven't seen him for years," Monteath said. "I did go to school with him."

Pam stopped.

"Don't tell me you helped turn the windows

17

inside out," she said. "Or — "

"None of them," Monteath said. He smiled, with some detachment. "Not my dish of tea, I'm afraid." He paused. "In fact," he said, "I'm not certain I'll know him now when I see him. It's been — it must be a dozen years since I've seen him. Something of a surprise to get — " But he did not finish. Pam turned her head to show that she listened, but Arthur Monteath merely smiled. It was, Pam decided, a diplomatic smile, which was appropriate. Diplomacy was Mr. Monteath's business, if one could call it a business. There must have been many times in — how many years? she wondered — when it had been better to smile than to speak.

"You're back for a while?" Jerry asked, and to that Monteath shrugged. He said one never knew.

"Back for consultation," he said, as they started up the stairs which led to penthouse level. "May mean a new assignment. May not."

"You've been in London?" Jerry said.

"Among other places," Monteath said. He smiled again. "They get us around, y' know," he said.

They went up a flight of stairs to a landing, and to a quite ordinary door. Jerry reached around Pam to the bell-push. He touched it. For a moment there was no response. Then,

18

from behind the door, there was the scream of a woman in anguish — a woman on a rack, all hope abandoned. The scream rose and fell and rose again; Pamela, recoiling, stepped back against her husband, who took her shoulders. Arthur Monteath, who seemed to pale in the soft light of the landing, said, "My God!" The door opened, and a man stood before them, carrying his head under his arm. The carried head spoke, its lips moving. "Killed her, that's what," the head said. "Killed all of them." Then the scream was repeated. "Do you want to come in?" the head enquired, and bowed at them. Arthur Monteath, again, said, "My God."

"Mr. Wilmot is expecting us," Pamela North told the head, which said, "Then I suppose you'll have to come in."

The body which held the head stepped back and a plump man beamed at them across a small foyer. The plump man looked at three faces and laughed resoundingly. He held both hands against his chest and laughed. When he was able, the plump man said, "Gives you a start, doesn't it?" The scream came again, and came from a portable record player on a table just inside the door. "Turn it off, Frank," Byron Wilmot said. "Set it again."

The body put its head on a table, and moved to the record player. "Sees through his shirt front," Wilmot said. "Quite an effect, eh?"

He came across the foyer, then, holding out both hands. He said, "Delighted, Mrs. North, Mr. North," and then, heartily slapped Arthur Monteath on the back and said, as heartily, "Good old Artie." Monteath, for an instant, looked as if he doubted it, doubted everything. "How's the boy?" Wilmot demanded. "Good old striped-pants Artie?"

Monteath made a sound without words. Then he said, "Nice to see you, Wilmot." He paused. "Quite a welcome," he added, and was told he hadn't seen the half of it. Wilmot then seemed to encircle the three of them, absorbing them across the foyer, into a big, oblong room with three sides almost altogether of glass. There were many people in the room. Some danced to music which seemed to pour from the solid wall; others stood with drinks, sat with drinks. They were people to be met.

They were met. They had names; they smiled; they were delighted — and Pam North was delighted, and Jerry charmed and Arthur Monteath suave. He's remembering all the names, Pam thought, and I'm not and Jerry isn't. There was a man named Jenkins (or Jameson?) who said to Pam, "I've heard of you, haven't I?" and a pretty, dark girl in a strapless white dress — could her name really be Writheman? — who said, "Dear Mr. Wilmot gives such wonderful parties, doesn't he?" But the man who might be named Jenkins did not wait to be told whether he had heard of Mrs. North and the girl said, "Oh Tommy, of *course*" before Pam could agree that Mr. Wilmot seemed to, certainly, and was gone to Tommy for a dance.

The man named Frank, who was now wearing his own inconspicuous head, was beside Pamela North with a tray of filled glasses and thrust it at her. Then as she said, "Scotch and water, please," the tray seemed to slip from his fingers and the glasses cascaded to the green-tiled floor. But from the floor they merely bounced, their contents no more liquid than Frank's carried head had been his own. Everybody laughed, except one gray-haired woman who gasped and seemed about to scream. But then she smiled instead.

Mr. Wilmot laughed harder than anyone. His pink face became a red face with merriment. But he said, "Get some real drinks, Frank."

"Get 'em yourself, Wilmot," Frank said, but that was funny, too, and Frank did get the drinks. Jerry's was in a glass which, whatever one did, dribbled its contents to the chin and Monteath's glass appeared to be melting drunkenly to one side. Both smiled politely

21

and made the best of things.

"To all fools," Wilmot said, holding up his glass, raising his voice. " 'Laugh and the world laughs — ' "

But the world did not laugh. There was the woman's scream again, rising in agony over the many voices, over the music, and there was nothing funny in the scream. No knowledge that an actress had once mimicked agony to make a record, that the record was on a turntable which pressure on a bell-push actuated, made the anguished cry a cause for laughter. For an instant it seemed to transfix those in the room. The dancers broke step, caught at uneasy balance. Glasses raised to lips were checked there; voices broke off as if speech were brittle.

This held only a moment, while everyone remembered. By then Wilmot was beaming at all of them, was telling Frank that he would get it, was crossing the living room to the foyer.

The dancers returned to dancing, but with heads turned toward the foyer. Those not dancing, talked and drank again, but waited too, only half listening to what was said. From the foyer, the scream was cut to silence and the resounding laughter of Mr. Byron Wilmot replaced it. Nothing, Pam North thought — nothing in the world — could be comic enough to match such laughter. As if knowing itself outdone, unheard, the music stopped and those who were dancing stopped with it. For an instant one voice went on against the off-stage laughter. A woman's voice said, " — would be the best joke of — " and then the speaker heard her lonely voice and the voice died.

"So you're at it again," a man's voice which was not Wilmot's said from the foyer. "I might have known you would be."

There was anger in the voice; it was as if the voice went naked in bitterness. Speaking so, not knowing how many heard him, the speaker was exposed, defenseless, and Pamela North, to defend him, spoke to Monteath, saying something, anything — that through the wide windows of the penthouse one beautifully saw New York. But Wilmot's laughter surged again and, when it ended, Wilmot said, "Joke's on you, eh? Thought you were — " But then a needle clicked on a record somewhere and the high-fidelity system hurled music through the living room, so that what Wilmot said further was lost in the rush of sound. As if that had been a signal, conversation began again in the crowded room.

But Pam North and Monteath — Jerry was somewhere else; Jerry was talking to the gray-haired woman who had almost screamed when the glasses fell — did not talk again. Monteath, for the moment without diplomacy, had turned toward the door from the foyer, and Pam, after looking up at him for a moment, turned too. Monteath's eyes were narrowed a little; he openly waited, listened without pretense. Pam listened too, and the man who was not Wilmot said, "Sure I'll stay. You bet I'll stay."

Then a slight tall man in his twenties — a man with a thin white face and black hair — came out of the foyer with Wilmot behind him. In the doorway, Wilmot put a plump hand on the younger man's shoulder and the man turned his head momentarily and looked at the hand. Wilmot left it there. Wilmot beamed past him and, seeing them watching, beamed at Pam North and Arthur Monteath. He seemed to propel the black-haired man toward them. The man had not dressed for the party. He wore a gray suit, the jacket open. One end of a narrow blue tie dangled below the other. Wilmot put his other hand on the thin man's other shoulder and guided him to Pam North.

"Want you to meet my nephew," Wilmot said, over the other. "Clyde Parsons, Mrs. North. This is Mrs. North, Clyde. Mrs. *Gerald* North." Having said this, Mr. Wilmot chuckled. "Have to get the boy a drink. Quite a shock he's had. Oh — this is Arthur Monteath, Clyde. Thought I was dying, he says."

Wilmot's plump hands offered Clyde Parsons to Pam North, to Monteath. Mr. Wilmot himself departed.

"Sorry," Parsons said. His voice was low, now. "He took me in — again." He pulled his coat together, buttoned it. His fingers went to his tie. "Not dressed for this," he said.

There was little to say to that and Clyde Parsons did not wait.

"I didn't know anything about all this," Parsons said. He was plainly uneasy, anxious to explain. "Got a message he was sick. Wanted to see me. Fix things — " He stopped and shook his head. Black hair fell over his forehead. He pushed it back. "One of his jokes," he said. "His damn funny jokes."

"Your uncle likes jokes," Pam said. This is really too embarrassing, Pam thought. Clyde Parsons looked at her as if she had not spoken what she thought.

"Sorry," he said. "I guess it's funny. Anyway, it's not your worry, is it? I — "

But Wilmot was back. He had a drink in his hand and held it out to Parsons; told Parsons to drink up, said it would do Parsons good. Parsons looked at the glass, for a long moment looked over it at Wilmot. Then with a movement oddly abrupt, Parsons took the glass and drank from it, thirstily. Almost at once, color came to his pale face.

"Take you around," Wilmot said, and put a hand again on his nephew's shoulder. Parsons seemed to hesitate. Then he drank from the glass again and said, "Why not, Uncle Byron?" in a different voice. "Have fun," Wilmot told Pam North and Monteath, and pushed Parsons from them.

"Well," Monteath said. "Wilmot hasn't — " He stopped. He looked down at Pam North and smiled, faintly. " — hasn't changed much," he said. "Tough on the kid."

"You know him?" Pam said.

"Of him," Monteath said. "Wouldn't you like to dance?" The change of subject was final. They danced.

It was not for some time, then, more than a moderately odd party. It was true that Frank, the comic butler, was at intervals unbridled, but as time passed his production of curious food and drink, his gay insults, his employment of a succession of improbable dialects, became, through repetition, almost commonplace. The music continued to pour from the concealed speaker; Frank, however impishly, continued to provide whatever was desired that had alcohol in it. It occurred to Pam, after an hour or so, that she was drinking more than she commonly did — which after dinner was commonly nothing at all — but this was partly because, as the evening progressed, it was Wilmot's whim to serve all drinks in glasses with rounded bottoms. It is difficult to mislay a drink in a round-bottomed glass.

There were, as Pam had anticipated, rubber spiders from time to time. Mr. Wilmot, while dancing with her — rather bouncingly — abruptly acquired a green lizard (of which he seemed unaware) and the lizard ran up and down his arm. It was true that, while ostensibly making a note of something, Mr. Wilmot produced a fountain pen which, apparently by accident, squirted a substantial stream of black fluid on Jerry North's white shirt front. But it was also true that, not long after Jerry's sharp yelp of unhappiness, the black stain faded gradually until it was hardly perceptible. (It was further true that, some weeks later, a faint brown stain remained where black had been, as a memento of a somewhat strange evening — and of Mr. Byron Wilmot.)

But after the arrival of Clyde Parsons, nothing really out of the way occurred for rather more than an hour. Then the scream of anguish came again from the foyer.

It was little noticed, this time. By some, indeed, it apparently was not heard. (Loquacity had become advanced; the scream had competition.) Pam and Jerry, who were dancing together for the first time, were only half conscious of the sound, although, as they circled, Pam saw Wilmot — he was really very pink now, particularly at the back of the neck — go toward the foyer. A moment later, his laughter roared and then, almost at once, he followed two people into the room.

Inside the door the two stopped and the hag put two slim hands up to a hideously unsightly face. But Wilmot was behind them, a hand between the shoulder blades of each, and the young man in rompers and short white socks, lollipop in hand, and the woman with a great hooked nose, coarse white hair streaming in disorder from beneath conical cap, were propelled into the room. The music did stop, then, and Wilmot raised his voice.

"Want everybody to meet these two," Wilmot shouted, and shouted through laughter. "Baker the boy wonder. The bewitching Miss Evitts." He stepped from behind them, and struck himself on the chest with both fists, and his laughter roared. "Seems they got the idea they were supposed to come as something," he told everyone, and was helpless with mirth.

Baker (the boy wonder) was not. He had a pleasant, rounded face and, as he stood before the party, ridiculous as a chubby small boy, his face was very red — very red and, possibly, very furious. The hand holding the lollipop seemed about to rise as if, absurdly, the lollipop might be a weapon. But then his free hand went out and around the shoulders of the woman.

She was a young woman, not the crone she seemed. The black witch's gown could not hide completely the youthful roundness of her body, although the enormous false nose and the lined grease paint burlesqued her face. And even at a distance, even with the man's arm on her shoulders, it seemed to Pam North that the woman's slender body trembled. Among those who looked at the two, someone laughed, a little hysterically.

"Mr. Wilmot," Jerry North said, in Pam's ear, "is a first grade bastard."

Pam said, "The poor things," and moved out of Jerry's arms toward them, but after she had taken a step Jerry held her. "It'll only make it worse," Jerry said. Perhaps he was right, she thought, and let herself be stopped.

The man in boy's clothing managed to laugh, then. He managed to say, "Guess the joke's on us, Mr. Wilmot," in a tolerably controlled voice. "You took us in, all right."

Wilmot laughed again at this, and slapped Baker on the shoulder. "That a boy," Wilmot said. "Get yourselves something to drink. Get Frank to fix you up."

The woman shook her grotesque head at first, but Baker's arm tightened on her shoulders. He bent and whispered to her and after a time she nodded. She went, then, apparently knowing her way, to a corridor at the end of the room — a corridor, Pam had by then discovered, which led to bathrooms. Baker stood for a moment watching her, and then Pam did cross the few feet to him — moved to him impulsively and got at first a blank look and then a slow, rueful smile.

"I think it was mean," Pam North said.

"Well," Baker said. "It's Mr. Wilmot. He told us it was a costume party, of course. Told us what to wear." He smiled again. "We both work for him, you see," he told her. "It's — " He stopped. Frank had appeared with a drink. Baker thanked the comic butler, took the glass with some apparent suspicion, sipped from it, started to put it down and looked at it again. "Oh," he said. "One of those." He sipped, his eyes on the far end of the room. Anger hardened his face again.

Jerry came up, wearing the expression of a man who thinks it time to go home, and began, "Don't you think, Pam — " and stopped because Pam touched his arm. Miss Evitts came out of the distant corridor and toward them up the long room. She wore the witch's dress still, but conical cap, gray hair, hooked nose were gone. Baker's face changed; anger went out of it and a kind of warm pleasure came into it and, as she approached them, Miss Evitts smiled too. It was a gentle smile; it was also, Pam North thought, a hurt smile.

She could be hurt, Pam thought — she could easily be hurt. There was gentleness in her face and sensitivity. Her hair, with the wig gone, was brown — a kind of gentle brown, Pam thought. Her eyes seemed very large. She flushed when she was introduced to the Norths. Her slender hands were busy with the stuff of the shapeless black dress. She was Martha Evitts. She was Mr. Wilmot's secretary. "He told us to wear — these things." She was not beautiful; perhaps she was not even pretty. She must, Pam thought, be in her quite late twenties; she might, at a guess, be two or three years older than Baker, who looked at her and seemed to see a beauty others did not see.

They're sweet, Pam thought, and Mr. Wilmot is all Jerry called him. In her own mind, which she did not pretend was especially innocent, Pam North thought of several adjectives which Jerry might have used to qualify a noun.

But at the same time, she qualified her earlier opinion of Byron Wilmot. She had thought him merely — well, underdone; thought him merely the doughy enlargement of a small boy who, on some long ago April Fool's Day, had persuaded other small boys to nibble at caramels made of laundry soap. But it appeared he was more formidable than that, and more possessed of malice. If Martha Evitts was in any danger of forgetting that she was a few years older than the man who so unguardedly loved her, Mr. Wilmot would see that the danger was lessened. She was aged crone; Baker was rompered child. It makes me a little sick, Pam thought, and turned to Jerry and said, "I think maybe we'd better be — "

But then a woman cried out. It was not this time the recorded scream from the phonograph in the foyer. It was at once less agonizing and more real. The pretty, dark girl in the white dress stood in the center of the dance floor, and pointed toward a french door leading to the terrace and said a long *"Oh-h-h-h!"* as if she were scared out of her pretty wits.

Beyond the door there was a man. His hat was pulled down to hide his face. He held an automatic in his right hand. The gun was a black finger, pointing death.

II

Wednesday, 11:46 P.M. *to*
Thursday, 2:40 A.M.

The man on the terrace, although he must have heard the cry, did not move. But there was no lack of movement in the big room. Movement was convulsive, jumbled together. Pam found herself in Jerry's hands, swirling as she was jerked behind him; Baker reached Martha Evitts and pulled her down to the floor; the gray-haired woman, at one moment dignified (and apparently a little sleepy) was the next on the floor, too, clutching at a chair, trying to pull it as a shield between her and the french door. A man shouted and began to run, dragging a woman with him and —

It was all very confused, Pam thought, looking around Jerry. It was as if someone had suddenly poured hot water on an ant hill.

The lights, except for two lamps at the far end of the room, went out, but the music continued playing Cole Porter's "Little Rhumba Numbah." In the semi-darkness, Jerry was brushed by someone hurrying and the Norths staggered momentarily.

The man on the terrace was only a shadow

now, but he did not seem to have moved.

Wilmot went past them, running, and he held a revolver in each hand and then he was yelling, "Get down, everybody. Get down."

But those who were not already down, merely looked at him, as if they did not understand what he was saying. People were not behaving very well, Pam thought, and spilled what remained in her highball glass on Jerry's trouser leg. Jerry jumped and said, "For God's sake, Pam, I — "

But now Mr. Wilmot, who had not got down himself, was in the center of the area set off for dancing — was a large, but unmistakable shadow there, holding a weapon in either hand. He turned from side to side, looking for something — for someone. Then he reached out, but not toward the man nearest him, and thrust one of the guns toward the man he selected.

"*Here!*" he said. "Take it, Artie. Got to get him before — " He made a gesture with the gun, toward the terrace.

Arthur Monteath seemed to hesitate. Then he took the gun. Wilmot said something to him which Pam could not hear, and then gestured violently toward his right. Monteath said, "I think it's — " and did not finish, but went in the direction Wilmot had indicated, holding the gun ready.

"*Sit tight!*" Wilmot shouted. "*Everybody sit tight! We'll get him!*"

"But Jerry," Pam said, "it's all so — "

"Yes," Jerry said, his voice low, an odd note in it. "I don't get it either."

The shadow beyond the french door was no longer visible. The man had run for it, of course. He had got away, of course. This was all farce, this was the unbelievable burlesque chase of an early movie, this was Keystone Cops.

Wilmot was running — although it was more of a trot than a run — toward a french door at his left.

"Going to get him between them," Jerry said. "I suppose that's what they're up to."

"He won't be there," Pam said. "Don't they know he won't be there? And anyway, if he's between them and everybody has a gun — don't they know *anything?*"

The music stopped. In the silence, there was the sound of a door opening toward one end of the room. That would be Arthur Monteath. A moment later, another door opened, toward the opposite end of the room. That would be Wilmot, encircling.

"*Jerry!*" Pam said. "*They're crazy! They — *"

"*There he goes!*" Wilmot shouted from the terrace. "*Get him, Artie! Stop, you, or I'll — *"

35

There was a shot, then. It seemed loud enough to be in the room. Through the glass there was a flash, reddish in the semi-darkness. Almost simultaneously, there was a second report and a second instantaneous flash and then Wilmot shouted again — shouted, *"Stop, I tell you! You can't — "*

There was the sound of at least one man running and then the sound stopped. There was a moment of silence and then Wilmot spoke again. He did not shout; the excitement had gone out of his voice, and something else had taken its place. But he spoke loudly. They could hear him through the glass.

"My God, Artie," Wilmot said. "You've killed the guy!"

Then the lights came on. Through the glass of the french doors the light flooded onto the terrace.

Wilmot was standing, his revolver lowered, over a figure lying on the terrace tiles. And, slowly, Monteath walked toward them, another revolver dangling in his hand.

Those in the room surged toward the terrace doors, then, jostled toward them. Wilmot looked up, as someone wrenched open the doors nearest him.

"All we wanted to do — " he began, and then Monteath spoke. He did not speak loudly; his voice was low and hard, but it carried.

"You said they were blank loads, Wilmot," Monteath said. "You said — "

Wilmot sat back on his heels and looked up at Monteath. Wilmot did not say anything. He reached down to the figure on the floor and then, for the first time, Pam North realized the figure was masked. Slowly, deliberately, Wilmot pulled off the mask.

The face was thin and white and for a moment Pam thought that the man who lay there was the thin, white youth Wilmot had called his nephew. But, in almost the same instant, she realized that she was wrong. The man on the terrace floor had red hair. Through one eyebrow ran a narrow scar. It wasn't Clyde Parsons — it wasn't anybody she had seen before.

Arthur Monteath looked down for a long moment at the face of the man he had shot. Then he looked, with a strange concentration, at the face of Wilmot, who was looking up at him. And then two strange things happened, or Pam thought they did.

She could not be sure that Wilmot, just perceptibly, nodded to Monteath. But of the next thing, she could be sure — they could all be sure.

Wilmot teetered back on his heels, caught himself with his hands, sat on the floor. And then Byron Wilmot laughed. Byron Wilmot

37

roared with merriment.

It was shocking for only a moment. Then it was obvious. What was on the floor was only the replica of a man. The red on the shirt came from one of Wilmot's ingenious devices. The —

"Ho, ho, HO!" Wilmot laughed. "Ha-ha, ha-ha, WHOAH!"

Someone in the group who looked down at him laughed. But it was nervous laughter. Another tried to laugh, and then another. Wilmot laughed on.

Arthur Monteath did not laugh at all. He stood, rather rigid, and looked down at Wilmot and Wilmot, red of face, leaned back on his hands and laughed up at him. He seemed, Pam thought, to laugh for Monteath.

It lasted only a moment. Wilmot got to his feet then, and his laughter died away. After a moment he reached down and took the mannequin by the coat collar and dragged it into the room.

In the room, except for the face, it was merely a clothing dummy. But even in the light, the face was surprising. It was not a face well-shaped and meaningless, the conventional mask of a face. It was individualized — a thin face, with slightly twisted lips. The wig which crowned the mannequin — and was now somewhat askew — was a wig of red hair, unnaturally smooth, to be sure, but losing by that nothing of its incongruity. Clothing dummies just don't have red hair, Pamela North thought. Why would anybody go to the trouble?

"Lifelike, ain't he?" Wilmot said. He turned to Monteath, who had come into the doorway and stood looking down at the plastic face. "Hell, Artie," Wilmot said. "Sure they were blanks. Think I want you banging away in my direction?" Monteath said nothing. "Hell, man," Wilmot said, "you can take a joke, can't you?"

Monteath spoke then, after a further pause.

"Why yes, Wilmot," he said. "I can take a joke." He paused and looked again at the mannequin's face. "You did a very convincing job," he said.

"Well," Wilmot said, "so did you, old man. So did you." He paused. "Know what I mean?" he said, making the meaningless phrase more meaningless with a chuckle. Monteath did not chuckle in return; he did not speak. He merely nodded.

The murder of the dummy was the climax of the evening. Mr. Wilmot did, to be sure, explain it all — how the dummy had been rigged to wires and so made movable, how Frank had been primed to turn off the lights at the appropriate moment, how Wilmot had had the blank-loaded revolvers ready to hand; how he had fired first, hoping that Monteath, thinking the man between had fired at them, would himself fire by reflex, knowing he would not kill.

"Had to get a man who would *do* something," Wilmot explained. "That's good old Artie."

If good old Artie appreciated this compliment, his face did not reveal it. Good old Artie laid down the gun, moved farther into the big living room, away from Wilmot, from the prostrate dummy.

Mr. Wilmot explained it all, being evidently pleased with all of it. He was listened to with politeness, rather than with avidity, and when he had finished, or nearly finished, his guests began to make the discovery that it was growing late. A fine party, a wonderful party. But tomorrow — no, today — was a working day. The blond girl and her Tommy were the first actually to leave, although there was nothing about either to suggest there were alarm clocks in their lives. Thereafter, there was a general collection of wraps, a series of congregations in the foyer — and not all Wilmot's jovial assertion that it was early yet, not all his proffer of newer tricks and more elaborate treats could stay the departing guests.

But Pam and Jerry North, although they had been among the first to think of leaving, were not among the first to leave. Jerry had, at what should have been a final moment, managed to get himself entrapped in conversation (with the gray- haired woman who had dropped so quickly behind a chair and who seemed to have been startled into complete wakefulness) and even after Pam had retrieved her stole (quite enough wrap for the rigors of the elevator) he had still not fully edged away.

So they, and Jerry's conversationalist and Arthur Monteath — who had been drawn aside by Wilmot himself, and who had listened rather than talked — and Baker in his romper suit and Martha Evitts in her weeds were on hand for the final act of the evening. The act was brief, and not pleasant.

Clyde Parsons came from some shadow. He came staggering. His too narrow tie was pulled to one side, his too pale face was now almost frighteningly white. He swayed as he stopped in front of his uncle and Monteath, as he — with drunken emphasis, looked Wilmot up and down.

"You're a bloody old fool," he said then, and said it loudly. "You can take your lousy money and — "

Wilmot stopped him, or at any rate drowned out his voice.

"You're drunk, Clyde," Wilmot said, his voice booming. "Drunk as usual." He smiled still, but there was no smile in his voice. "Get the hell out of here," he said. "Frank!"

But there was no need for Frank. Clyde Parsons got himself out of there and his destination, Pam thought as he wavered past her, might well be that indicated. There was hell enough in his thin, pale face. He wavered into the foyer.

He was at the outer door when the gray-haired woman caught up with him, detained him momentarily. She turned back to look at Wilmot, and she said, flatly, "You do things well, don't you, Byron? Nobody does them better, do they?"

And then she went, with Parsons.

"Good night," Baker said then, and said it abruptly, and Martha Evitts said nothing, and did not look at Wilmot and went with Baker. "Sorry about that," Wilmot said. "We've had a good deal of trouble with Clyde. Nice boy, but he will — "

"It's been," Pam North said, "a very interesting party, Mr. Wilmot." She paused. "So much going on," she said, and then she went and Jerry after her.

The elevator door closed when they were

just in sight of it. The elevator carried down-ward, presumably, Parsons and the woman with gray hair, Baker in his rompers and Miss Evitts in dusty black.

"Who," Pam asked, while they waited, "was your talkative friend?"

"Talkative?" Jerry said. "Oh. You didn't meet her?"

"Anyway," Pam said. "She didn't stick. I mean — "

"Yes," Jerry said. "Well, that was Mrs. Wilmot. The Mrs. Wilmot who used to be. She divorced Wilmot because he put a snake in her bed."

"Annoying," Pam said. "But still."

"It wasn't rubber," Jerry said. "It was — "

"Good heavens!" Pam North said. "A *snake* snake?" Jerry nodded. "Divorce was too good for him," Pam said. "It's coming now."

It was, by its rumble. There was only the sound to prove its progress; the indicator arrow pointed stubbornly to the fifth floor, as it had for a week or more.

Arthur Monteath joined them while they still waited. He said, "Quite a party." He looked, Pam North thought, tired, and older than he had looked a few hours before.

"Phew!" Jerry said.

The elevator door opened and they went into the little box.

"Why," Pam said, when the elevator started down, "don't you stop in and have a drink? Now, I mean. Unless you don't like cats, of course."

"I do like cats," Monteath said. "But isn't it rather — "

"Not really," Pam said. "And how can anybody sleep after — after all that? Can you, Jerry?"

Jerry North thought he might; thought he very easily might. But he did not say this. Monteath hesitated. Then he said, "I'd like to. For only a few minutes, I promise," thus somewhat surprising both of the Norths.

They stopped. Drinks were suggested, coffee was agreed upon. The cats awoke; they smelled Arthur Monteath, who put a hand close to the floor so that it might be smelled conveniently; who was accepted at once by Sherry, partially accepted by Gin, rejected — but without undue prejudice — by Martini who, when Pam finally sat down (humans wasted more time) occupied Pam's lap, from that safety to stare at Monteath with the roundest of blue eyes.

Conversation was not active. Monteath was in New York for a few days only, going then to Washington. He would telephone Jerry before he left and arrange an appointment to discuss the ambassador's book. Where the

44

world went from where it was, no good place, was anybody's guess. Monteath was abstracted, the major part of his mind clearly elsewhere.

"Mr. Wilmot certainly goes to a lot of trouble," Pam said at one point. "Why a special face on the dummy?"

"Why any of it?" Jerry said. "What an evening!"

"An — an inventive man," Monteath said, of Wilmot, but let it drop there. Sherry rubbed against his leg and he stroked her, absently. Then he stood up, quite suddenly. He would, he said, be getting along. He appreciated the coffee. He smiled, then, and the smile changed his face.

"The fact is," he said, "I'm keeping us all up."

The protest was only polite. They went with him to the door, waited until the elevator came, the door closed and the mechanism ground.

"There wasn't much point to that, was there?" Jerry enquired, and yawned and undid his tie. "What was all that about not being able to go to sleep?"

Pamela said she didn't know, and yawned too. It had been an idea, only an idea; not a good idea. Of course, she added, there was always the ambassador's book. But to that Jerry, coatless, removing studs from his shirt,

45

said only, sleepily, "Huh," dismissing all books by all ambassadors.

Yet they were too sleepy, too tired, to hurry into bed. In robes, they drifted back to the living room, sleepily they drank more coffee, which did not arouse them. The cats suggested activities. Martini brought a battered catnip mouse, urging that it be thrown, and Jerry threw it, feebly.

"Why don't we go to bed?" Pam asked. "Wake up and go to bed?" and absently poured herself the remaining half cup of not hot coffee. Jerry didn't know; he said he didn't know, and did not move. Then nobody said anything and then Jerry began to breathe deeply.

That sufficiently aroused Pam, who sufficiently aroused Jerry. But they still went to their beds without opening the window and Pam was just experiencing a pleasant blurring of thought when she remembered.

She went to the window, from which one could look down to a quiet street, and raised it wide.

And then, because of what she saw, she drew her breath in quickly and then cried out, *"Jerry! Jerry!"*

"Wha—What!" Jerry said, coming out of sleep. *"What!?"*

"Something just fell by," Pam said. "Some-

thing — *Jerry, it was a man!* Jerry — *somebody fell out!*"

She had turned from the window.

"Jerry," she said. *"I think it was Mr. Wilmot!"*

There was a group already there. The superintendent of the building was there, with his wife, who hugged around her a robe she filled without shaping. Several people had come out of nowhere to form a circle, and more came. Then the police came in a prowl car. They came simultaneously with the Norths, who had had to dress — who had hesitated to come at all, being people who gave wide berth to street accidents, hurrying past them, with Pam always a little white. But if it is callous to stare in curiosity it is also callous to say, in effect, "Oh, Mr. Jones just went by" as Mr. Jones falls past your bedroom window. "Particularly," Pam North pointed out, "if he's just been your host."

Why she was so certain the man who had fallen was — or now, more accurately, had been — Byron Wilmot, Pam could not explain to Jerry as, after waiting a moment for the elevator, they ran down the stairs. "I know there wasn't time to tell," Pam said. "But — who else would it have been?"

One of the policemen looked at what was

47

on the sidewalk. The other said, "All right, now. Stand back," and then, "Anybody here named North?"

There was, Jerry admitted.

"You made the squeal? That is, you telephoned?"

"Yes," Jerry said.

"Yeah," the policeman said. "You telephoned. Said a man had fallen."

"Somebody," Jerry said. "My wife thought it was a man."

"Oh," the policeman said. "She did, huh? You his wife?"

"Yes," Pam said.

"O.K.," the policeman said. "So you'd better have a look. Let these people through there."

But Pam shrank back, shaking her head. Jerry, feeling a little sick, went through the circle. He looked at what was on the sidewalk. He said, "My God!"

The dummy was fragments, strewn widely. There was nothing left of the face over which someone had taken such pains. If the red wig had not been among the shards, if one arm had not escaped disintegration, it would have been difficult to tell what had been shattered on the sidewalk.

"Quite a joke, mister," the articulate policeman said. "Very funny joke. Ever think it might have hit somebody? Ever hear there's a law against throwing things out windows?"

It wasn't, Jerry explained, their joke. They had reported only what had happened, or what they thought had happened.

"Look, Ben," the cop who had been staring at the remains said, "whata we do with it?"

Ben pondered this.

"Of course," he said, "the ambulance boys'll be along." He did not say this with confidence. He offered it with doubt.

"Trouble is," the other policeman said. "It's not a body, is it? But on the other hand, it's something like a body." He looked at it. "Was," he said.

"I tell you," Ben said. "It's litter." He looked around the circle, which was by way of becoming a crowd. *"You!"* he said. "You the janitor?"

"Superintendent," the woman in the robe said. "Tell him, Lennie. Don't let him push you around."

Lennie was a small man.

"That's right," he said. "Superintendent." He paused. "Officer," he added.

"You know what this is, don't you?" Ben demanded, in the voice of a policeman. "What you got here's a violation. Ordinance — what's the ordinance, Charlie?"

"Littering the sidewalk, multiple dwelling,"

the other patrolman said. "Number — I don't know the number offhand. Also, throwing things out of windows to the public danger. Also — "

The ambulance came then, its lights red. It stopped and panted and an interne came out on one side and the driver on the other.

"We live in the basement," Lennie said, and his voice quavered. "This came down from up."

"What the?" the interne said, looking at the remains of the dummy. He waved his hand at it. "What the?"

"That gentleman," Ben said, and looked at Jerry North with sternness. "Said a man jumped or fell."

"Defenestration," Pam North said, unexpectedly, her voice rather high. "If people would just be quiet, we'd tell you. It's Mr. Wilmot's."

The patrolman named Ben took his cap off. He rubbed his head. He replaced the cap.

"Listen, lady," Ben said. "*That's* Mr. Wilmot?" He shook his head. "Friend of yours, probably?" he said. "Friend of hers, Charlie."

"Ha," the other patrolman said.

"Mr. Wil*mot's*," Pam said. "He lives in the penthouse. There was a party and somebody

50

shot — this." She pointed. "It was his idea of a joke."

"His?" Ben said, and indicated the fragments.

"Listen," the ambulance interne said, "what the? You expect us to take this?"

"Put a D.O.A. tag on it, doc," the driver of the ambulance said. "That's what they want. D.O.A. tag. Then we go get some coffee."

There was a siren around the corner. A prowl car came around the corner behind red lights. It joined the ambulance and the first prowl car. Two men, one of them rather drunk, came around the corner after it. Across the street, several people opened windows. A sergeant got out of the new prowl car and said, loudly, "All right. What's going on here?" He looked around. "You, McGillicuddy," he said. "What's all this?"

"You got me, sergeant," Ben McGillicuddy said. "This was supposed to be a man." He pointed.

"By whom?" the sergeant said, in a voice heavy with skepticism.

"I've been trying — " Pam said.

"Always push you around, Lennie," the superintendent's wife said.

"Those two," Patrolman McGillicuddy said, and pointed. "They made the squeal."

"Leave us get the hell out of here, doc,"

the ambulance driver said. "We can't take *that* in."

"All right," the sergeant said. "What's it all about, lady? What's the name, lady?"

"North," Jerry said. "If you'd let us — "

"Listen," the sergeant said. "*Gerald* North? Mr. and Mrs. *Gerald* North?"

"All right," Jerry said. "Yes."

"My God!" the sergeant said.

"I've been trying to tell this — this officer," Pam said. "It belonged to Mr. Wilmot. He must have — have dropped it." She paused. "After all," she said. "It's April Fool's Day. Or just was."

"Wait a minute," the sergeant said. He said, "All right, doc, nothing for you." He said, "Get this broken up, McGillicuddy." He took a deep breath. "All right," he said. "Go ahead, Mrs. North."

Pamela North went ahead.

All manner of things happen to policemen. Sergeant Fox thought this, getting out of the elevator on the twelfth floor, searching for and finding the flight of stairs to the penthouse. At two-thirty in the morning (not even of April Fool's Day) he was required to ask a man named Wilmot why he had dropped a clothing dummy thirteen stories to a sidewalk, to the hazard of pedestrians — to ask him

52

what kind of joke he thought that was. It seemed rather silly.

Sergeant Fox reached the landing and found a door. He found a bell-push. Remembering what Mrs. North — and wait until he told Mullins he had finally met the Norths, under circumstances as screwy as were to be expected — remembering what Mrs. North had told him, Sergeant Fox braced himself for a woman's scream. But he heard, instead, melodious chimes. He waited, heard nothing more, pushed again. He pushed several times.

"Wha's the matter," a thick voice said, finally. It came closer to the door. "Wha's going on, eh?"

"Police," Fox said.

"Don' want any policeman," the voice said. The voice was very fuzzy. Since it did not clear, Fox decided it was fuzzy with drink.

"I want to talk to you, Mr. Wilmot," Fox said. "It is Mr. Wilmot?"

"Don' wanta talk to *you*," the voice told him, fuzzier than before.

"You are Mr. Wilmot?"

"So I'm Mr. Wilmot. Go away."

"An — an object seems to have fallen," Fox said. "Apparently from your terrace."

"Keep it," the voice said. "Jus' keep it, captain."

"Listen," Fox said. "Open the door, will

you?" He tried the knob. The knob did not turn.

"Castle," the fuzzy voice said. "Home is my castle. Talk about it in the morning."

The trouble, Fox thought, was that Mr. Wilmot had something there, had a good deal there. He had, presumably, dropped a dummy from his terrace to the sidewalk. Listening to the voice, this seemed to Fox quite likely. He might have killed someone. But — he had not killed anyone. He had violated a city ordinance. But his penthouse remained his castle, short of a warrant for search, or a warrant for arrest. Fox could, of course, stick a summons under the door.

"You might have killed somebody," Fox said, to the door.

"Can' hear you."

"Killed somebody," Fox repeated.

"Didn't hit anybody," the fuzzy voice said. "Looked. Smashed the dummy, s'all."

"So you admit — "

"Go away," the voice said. "Wanna get some sleep. Talk about it in the morning. Accident, anyway. Damned thing cost money."

"You do admit — "

"Pushed it out on the terrace. Pushed it too far, s'all. Coulda happened to anybody."

"I'd still like — "

"Morning, keep telling you. Gotta make something of it, come 'round in the morning. Hear me?"

"Well — "

"That's a man," the voice said. "Morning, eh? Fix it all up in the morning. Pay the fine. Whatever it is. Gotta sleep now."

"Well," Fox said again.

It was not satisfactory. It left the report messy. But — if Wilmot did not want him in, he was not going to get in. Wilmot was, in any case, clearly in no condition to talk coherently. He probably had, further, told all he could ever remember — he had pushed the dummy onto the terrace; he had pushed it too far. It was all extremely silly.

"Somebody'll be around for a statement in the morning," Fox told the door.

There was no answer. It occurred to Fox that Wilmot had already gone back to bed. Fox went down the stairs, and down in the elevator. Anyway, somebody else would see Wilmot in the morning. Fox would be in bed himself.

III

Thursday, 10 A.M. *to* 11:35 A.M.

This would be the last time. That Martha
Evitts promised herself, and again pressed
the bell-push, heard again the melodious
chimes from within. She had let it drift too
long, and that was something she too often
did. It was because there is a kind of violence
about decision, and a violence which, at any
given moment, usually seems excessive to the
occasion. Such excessive violence becomes
melodrama, and demonstrates that one has
taken oneself too seriously, and so one becomes ridiculous, at any rate in one's own
eyes. But now, quite simply, she had had
enough.

There would be no need to say why, so to
reveal how seriously the whole ridiculous
business had affected her — so to reveal that
she could not, actually, "take a joke." There
was no reason to let him know that she knew
what he had been up to — no reason to take
an attitude about it, and lay herself open again
to being laughed at. Or even, which was
worse, pitied. She had been pitied last night
and, standing alone before an unopening door,

she flushed softly as she remembered. There had been sympathy, which was pity, in the eyes of the bright-haired woman named Mrs. North. It had been quick and warm and friendly, but that made it no better. Mrs. North had realized that she could not "take a joke" of this kind, although Mrs. North could hardly have realized the full implication of the "joke." But perhaps she had — perhaps they all had. Certainly, and that mattered most, John Baker had. That was of course what had been intended.

Probably it had spoiled things, which also probably had been intended. It had made it impossible — and it had all along, of course, been difficult enough for her — to accept this matter of a few years as a matter entirely trivial. It was, certainly; by any reasonable approach, it surely was. John had laughed about it, and she had believed his laughter, believed he thought it ridiculous of her to labor the matter of some three years and seven — no, eight, really — months. He had tried to laugh her out of it, and — part of the time — had almost succeeded. Almost he had persuaded her it was who you were, and how you felt, not a count of the days of your life, which mattered. He had been angry once, and the only time with her, when she had used an old phrase and a tired one — had said she would feel like a "cradle-snatcher." But he had ended by laughing, making her laugh with him.

But she had not, finally, been tough enough. A hundred young women — and twenty-nine was young; of course twenty-nine was young — would be tough enough, and good luck to them. She ought to be. She wasn't. Wilmot had seen that; had based his joke on that. He knew how to hurt, which is a knowledge as useful to the practical joker as to the wit. To the world's eyes, he said, she was an ancient crone, John Baker a boy in rompers. "Laugh at the fools," he had said. "Or be sorry for them. Let them see how they look to the rest of us."

They should have known; should have refused. But they had hardly thought of it, having expected safety in numbers. Everyone would be in some fashion absurd in costume; they would not be singled out; nobody would notice anything. Oh, it had been well planned enough. And between her and John it would always be an ugly thing. Coming as it had before they had achieved any sureness of each other, it might be an ineradicable thing. If they went on, they would always fear that some moment which should go on wings would flounder, weighted by the grotesque.

At least, Martha Evitts thought, reaching

in her bag for the key she was going to have to use, it would be that way with her. She could never hope again that any part of it might be perfect. Perhaps John would mind less, but even of that she was not sure. There had been an uncharacteristic hardness in him, when he took her home. The hardness underlay all the gentleness he showed toward her. So, no doubt, he realized, as she did, that things were spoiled. . . . Well, he had taught her to laugh at Wilmot's heavy, middle-aged approaches; Wilmot's suggestions of an "arrangement." They had laughed together, in that equally young together. Mr. Wilmot, however, had laughed last.

And now, for the last time, she was appearing dutifully at Mr. Wilmot's apartment to take dictation, provided with a door key for use in the event that Mr. Wilmot had gone out to breakfast and lingered over it. For the last time she would avoid Mr. Wilmot's words, and Mr. Wilmot's patting hands. For the last time she would pretend not to notice what he was about. And for the first time, she would tell him she had had enough. That —

No, she thought again, turning the key. What would be the use? She would tell him she had another offer, was going on to a job with a better future. There was no point in making the issue plain. There was no point, she thought, opening the door, in much of anything.

As Martha Evitts stepped into the foyer she hesitated, and looked around warily. This was almost automatic; in the foyer of Mr. Byron Wilmot's apartment, things often jumped at you. There was a strong possibility, this morning, that Mr. Wilmot might have a few tricks left over from the party, and would play them on her. But nothing jumped at her, nothing made alarming sounds at her, nothing slithered on the foyer floor. She took off her coat and hung it in the closet, made sure that her notebook was in her purse, unconsciously straightened her soft, brown hair. Then she went into the living room.

Just inside she stopped, as if she had walked into a wall. She put both slim hands up in front of her, as if to protect herself from the wall. And she thought, *No! This is too much. This is utterly too much.*

This time, presumably for her benefit, Mr. Wilmot had really gone to town. This time he had spared *no* effort, done *anything* for a laugh.

Mr. Wilmot, in a dressing gown and pajamas, lay on his back on the green-tiled floor. He lay there neatly, his arms by his sides, the dark blue of his robe smooth over

60

his rolling abdomen.

For some distance around the recumbent Mr. Wilmot, there was a shallow, dark expanse of what anyone — not knowing Mr. Wilmot — would have taken for blood. Sticking upright from Mr. Wilmot's chest was the haft of what anyone who did not know the Wilmot habits would have taken for a knife, its blade embedded. Versimilitude was complete; one could have sworn that Mr. Wilmot lay there murdered.

Having given the effect the tribute of a convulsive halt, Martha Evitts now gave it the further acknowledgement of a gasp of horror. (After all, much trouble had been gone to. Antagonistic as she felt toward Mr. Wilmot, she could not entirely let him down.) Momentarily, she waited for Mr. Wilmot to rise, to laugh, to tell her that he sure had fooled her that time.

When he did not rise (to take his bow), Martha decided that more was expected. A scream — at least a moderate scream — was indicated. Martha drew in breath to scream.

And with the breath she drew there came a kind of muskiness — something not quite a recognizable odor — something that made the nerves at the back of her neck tighten, as if she were a furred creature and the fur were lifting.

She did not scream. Her face drained white, her hands trembling before her face, she backed from the dead man — from the sweet muskiness of blood — from murder on a green-tiled floor.

For seconds she stood so, her hands shutting away the sight of Mr. Wilmot with a knife in his chest; her mind sickly accepting what her eyes had seen. She felt nausea beginning, and backed farther toward the foyer.

Then she not so much saw as became aware of in her nerves some movement in the room. She made herself take down her hands, and look beyond the body, across the room. She saw him then, for an instant.

John Baker was not in the room. He was on the terrace outside; she saw him, for that fraction of a second, through the glass of the french doors. She saw his face. He looked at her, across the dead man. Then, as if he had not seen her, he was gone.

She saw him so briefly, his movement from her vision was so flickeringly quick, that it was almost possible for her to think she had not seen him — that the shock of what she had seen, and now still saw, had somehow so jangled her perceptions as to wreck their reliability. But she could not really think this. John Baker had been on the terrace, looking into the room — looking at her without seeming to see her, at what was on the floor, at —

She stood, shuddering, and waited. A thought hammered at her mind. *At the man he had killed? At the man —*

She would not let the thought into her mind. John would not kill a man. (But last night he had been hard, bitter, not like himself.) John had come to the apartment before her (for what reason?) and had found what she had found. Something (but what? *What?*) had taken him to the terrace. He had looked in, but it was darker in the room. He had not seen her. (But the room was full of light.) Or — or he had gone to another door, he would come to her, tell why he had come to the penthouse, how he had found —

She waited. It seemed she waited for a long time, and as she waited her body shook. And John Baker did not come.

When she turned, the movement was almost convulsive in its quickness. But it seemed to her that the foyer was dark, and that she groped through it to the closet, then to the door, and that the hall outside was darker still. She stumbled on the stairs, and caught herself, and when she reached the elevator she pressed the bell and kept her finger on it long after the car had started up — kept pressing it with a kind of desperation.

John Baker swore to himself. Martha had not told him she was coming there that morning. Not, of course, that it would have made any real difference if she had, although he might somehow have stopped her. The other, he had not been able to stop. Things had got out of hand.

That she had seen him, he was almost certain, although she had looked so shocked standing there, so shaken, that it was hard to tell how much she had seen and taken in. It was, all around, a bad mixup. She would, of course, get onto the police before — well, before it was time for the police.

The whole thing had gone haywire. There wasn't much to be done about it. He watched, out of sight, until Martha had gone through the foyer and he waited, after that, for a few minutes longer. Then he went into the living room and began to work. He worked fast, and as he worked he listened.

He had had some five minutes, which was more time than he had counted on, when he heard someone at the foyer door. He had expected more warning than that. It was a near thing. But he was on the terrace, looking in, when Sylvester Frank entered the living room.

The butler — who now was only a slight man in his thirties, wearing a business suit

— stopped, too, as if he had run into something. But his face, from the distance at which John Baker stood, did not appear to change. He stopped; he looked at the body of his employer. There was, to be sure, a slight tremor of his body. It looked uncommonly like a shrug.

He stood for a moment, looking at the body. He walked around it, skirting the spreading blood. He stopped and looked around the room, and out through the doors, and Baker was out of sight, he hoped quickly enough. But he could not see without being seen. He waited a moment, and risked a quick look. Frank was at the telephone.

Whether Frank was calling the police or not — and Baker could only guess and wonder — there was at the moment nothing more to be done at the penthouse. Baker had done what he could; things had gone haywire. There was no immediate help for that.

There were more ways than one off the penthouse roof. Baker took one little frequented.

Pamela North had been sure there was another can of coffee. She had remembered distinctly that there was another can of coffee. She had known precisely where it was; it was where the coffee always was. It wasn't.

Jerry awakened to hear the news. Jerry groaned. He reported a headache.

"It's the most mysterious thing," Pam said. "I can just see it there. Yesterday afternoon."

"Oh *no!*" Jerry said.

She would, Pam North said, just go around the corner. It wouldn't take a minute.

"I'll get some clothes on," Pam said, and started to. For a time, Jerry watched her, gloomily. Then he groaned again, but with less assurance — this was a reminiscent groan. He swung out of bed, said, "Ouch!" and then that they might as well both go. They could drink their coffee and buy it too. In due course they went, sat at a counter, drank coffee and ate eggs. Jerry revived, but not excessively.

"I suppose," he said, after the second cup, "that *you* feel fine?"

"Yes," Pam said, simply.

Jerry looked at her. She looked fine. He groaned again, mildly. He said it was an unfair world.

"Why go to the office?" Pam asked. "Let illiteracy flourish."

Jerry was tempted. His conscience raised shocked hands. He would be no good anyway, Jerry told his conscience. His conscience shook its head. It isn't as if I had a hangover, Jerry told his conscience. I need sleep. "Pooh!" Jerry's conscience said. "Of course you have."

Jerry hailed a cab. Pamela bought coffee — also oranges, bacon which would turn out to have really been cured and could be returned if not (and which had not, and was not returned), English muffins, a dozen eggs and a jar of red caviar. These things she carried home, as penance. It was a bright morning; it was almost as if New York City might, for once, have spring. It was, Pam thought, too bad about Jerry and mornings. Mornings were fine.

The morning still was fine, although the grocery bag was beginning to grow heavy, when Pam went into the lobby of the apartment building. It was fine as, having pressed the signal button, she waited for Joe to bring the elevator down. It was fine until the elevator door opened.

A slim young woman, holding a cloth coat tight about her, came out of the elevator. Her face was very white, her lips moved, white teeth rubbing them; the eyes in her drained white face seemed inordinately large, and seemed tormented. Before she took this in, Pam North started to smile, remembering. This was the girl last night in the awful —

But the smile faded. The young woman did not appear to see Pam North. She did not appear to see anything. It seemed to Pam that the girl moved unsteadily, as if in partial darkness. She brushed past Pam and went toward the door and the street. When she was near the door she began almost to run. It was as if she were running in darkness, although she was in fact running toward the sun.

Pam had turned to watch her. She turned back, now, to Joe. Joe was looking after the hurrying girl, and his mouth was open.

"She sure acts scared," Joe said. "She's a girl works for Mr. Wilmot in the penthouse."

"She was — terrified," Pam said. "It was — something dreadful must have happened."

She made no move to get into the elevator. All the fineness had gone out of the morning. It was chilly in the lobby, by the elevator.

"All right a while ago," Joe said. "Comes maybe twice a week. Stenographer, I guess. Secretary or something. A little while ago I took her up and she was all right. Not chatty or anything, but all right."

Pam waited.

"Then she starts ringing," Joe said. "Just leans on the button, though I started fast as I could. I opened the door ready to ask where the fire was and there she was, looking like that. All the way down you could — well, sort of hear her breathing."

"Evitts," Pam said. "That's her name. Martha Evitts."

68

"Could be," Joe said. "Well — " He stood aside for Pam to go into the elevator.

"Something dreadful must have happened," Pam said again. But she went into the elevator.

"Say he's a great man for jokes," Joe said, closing the door, starting the car. "Booby trap jokes. Maybe — " He stopped the car. He said, "Here we are." He waited. Pam got out. She went into her apartment. She put the bag of groceries on a kitchen counter. She stood looking at it.

But Pam North was not looking at it. She was not looking at anything. She was seeing a sensitive face, working in terror — in shock. She was seeing the blankness in large eyes. She tried to erase the picture from her mind; spent minutes in the effort, and abstractedly stored groceries in refrigerator and in bins. But the picture held, grew more vivid. Pam gave up, then, and, certain she had already wasted priceless time, almost ran from the apartment, along the corridor to the elevator. It seemed that Joe would never come with the car. But he came. He opened the door.

"No," Pam said. "We can't just — do nothing." She looked at Joe, then. "You saw her face," she said. "She — people don't look like that unless — I don't know what. We've got to find out, Joe. Something's — awfully wrong."

"Now listen, Mrs. North," Joe said. "He's a tenant. We can't go barging — "

"So," Pam North said, "am I. You want me to walk up?"

Joe hesitated. He shrugged. He closed the door and started the car. At the twelfth floor he stopped the car and opened the door. Pam went out; went toward the stairs to the penthouse. Joe looked after her a moment. "Damn it to hell!" Joe said, and went after her.

Pam rang and chimes sounded. She waited and rang again.

"Like I said," Joe told her, relief in his voice. "Like I said, nobody's home."

"You didn't," Pam said, and tried the knob. It turned. She opened the door a crack, pressed the bell again, heard the chimes again, and then called through the crack of the door. "Anybody there?" Pam said. "Mr. Wilmot?"

"Look, Mrs. North," Joe said. "You can't do that. It's private."

But Pam already had. The door was open. She called again. She went into the foyer. Joe, torn between tenants, stood behind her in the open door. Pam went across the foyer and looked into the living room beyond. She gave a little, shuddering cry, and Joe crossed the foyer and looked over her. "Jeeze!" Joe said. He looked at Mr. Wilmot, on his back in

70

blood. "Whatta you know?" Joe said. "Whatta you know?"

Pam backed against him, backing away.

"Take it easy, Mrs. North," Joe said. "Just take it easy. Maybe it's one of his — "

"*No!*" Pam said. "Can't you see?"

Joe could see; he could see too well.

"I guess," he said, "we gotta call the cops." He started to go around Pam, into the room, in search of a telephone. But Pam stopped him. They should not go farther into the penthouse; they should not touch anything in the penthouse. "Come on," Pam North said, and led the way out. Joe went willingly.

"I'll call," Pam said, in the elevator, going down. "I — I know the right ones."

"Jeeze," Joe said. "Somebody sure — " He stopped speaking. At the fourth floor he stopped the car.

"Want me to — ?" he began, but Pam shook her head. She ran back to the apartment, and into it. Three cats stared. She said, quite politely, to the cats, "Don't bother mamma now," and went to the telephone. She dialed a number in the Watkins exchange and, when she was answered, said, "Can I speak to Captain Weigand, please?" as politely — as numbly — as she had spoken to the cats.

She heard a familiar voice. She said, "Bill, this is Pam," and gave him time only to

71

begin an answer.

"Bill," Pam North said, "I'm terribly sorry but — but I'm afraid I've found a body. With — with a knife in it." She paused; she swallowed. She saw blood spreading from a plump man, spreading on a green floor. "It's a Mr. Wilmot, Bill," she said. "There was a great deal of — "

She broke off. She waited a moment, and things got a little better.

"I think you'd better come, Bill," Pam said. "It's right here on top of the building."

She called Jerry, then. She felt he would want to know.

The block in front of the building was already filled with cars, with people, when William Weigand, acting captain, Homicide, Manhattan West, turned his Buick into it. He found a spot near enough the curb. Mullins got out on one side; Weigand on the other. By common impulse, they looked up, but not toward what Pam North had described as the top of the building. They looked toward windows on the fourth floor. Pamela and Gerald North, side by side, were leaning out of a window, looking down.

"This'll tie Arty in knots," Sergeant Aloysius Mullins said, referring to Deputy Chief Inspector Artemus O'Malley, bearing with fortitude the thought of Inspector O'Malley tied in knots. "There's that to be said for it, Loot I mean captain," Mullins said. He lifted a hand in salute to the Norths. "With the Norths in it," he added.

"It'll be screwy," Weigand finished for him, leading the way. "All right, sergeant."

They went among the curious, past uniformed men at the door of the apartment house, past a uniformed man in the lobby. They went up in the elevator, not stopping at the fourth floor. That would come later. They climbed the stairs to the penthouse.

It was surprising — it was always surprising — how so many men could get so little in one another's way. In the doorway from the foyer, Bill Weigand stopped for a moment, watching a scene with which he was long familiar. Mr. Wilmot's last party was well attended.

The precinct was, as usual, fully represented. The detective district — in this case the First, with headquarters at the Charles Street Station — had provided a three-man contingent, headed by Captain Rothman. The police photographers were at it, the fingerprint men were industriously dusting. There wasn't yet — Weigand moved into the room to let new arrivals enter — there was now an assistant district attorney from the Homicide Bureau and a detective from the same. "Hello, Flannery," Weigand said to the latter. Rothman came over. "M.E.'s not here yet," he said. He looked at Mr. Wilmot, still on his back, still wearing a black-handled knife in his chest. "Bled a lot, didn't he?" Rothman said. "How's Arty?"

"As usual," Weigand said.

Rothman expressed sympathy. He said it looked as if this — he indicated — had been dead quite a while. He said, "You know about him, don't you?"

"Right," Bill said. "By reputation."

"The playboy of the Western World," Rothman said. "Rather a nuisance in his early days."

"Well, the joke's on him this time. You got the squeal?"

"Friends of mine live in the building," Weigand said. The two watched. There was as yet nothing more required of them. Mullins, talking with a precinct man, wrote in his notebook. "People named North," Bill said.

"The ones who get in Arty's hair?"

"Right," Bill said. "He considers them — irregular. He — "

But then the man from the medical examiner's office came. He looked with distaste at the blood. He said, to the photographers, "You boys about through?" and one of the

74

photographers took just one more. The physician moved in, then. He looped a cord around the knife and drew it out. He looked around with it, and a man from the lab took it. The doctor examined; he took temperature; he probed the wound. Photographers shot elsewhere; elsewhere fingerprint men dusted. Overlooking all, a sketch-artist made a diagram. After a time the doctor stood up. He turned to Rothman and Weigand, and the assistant district attorney and the bureau detective joined them.

"Well," the doctor said. "He's dead enough. Got him in the heart or close to it. Lost consciousness within seconds; probably died within seconds. You want an estimate?"

"Right," Bill said. "The usual."

The doctor looked at his watch. It was twenty minutes past eleven.

"After midnight," the doctor said. "Before — oh, say six."

They waited. Dr. Foynes was a cautious man. He felt them waiting.

"Narrower?" he said.

"If you can, doctor," Bill said.

"Never give up, do you?" Foynes said. "All right — between two and four, at a guess. With margin of error as indicated. Death almost at once after the wound — probably. Didn't move around much — probably. Stabbed from in front by right-handed person — probably. Conceivably, from a quick look, he could have done it himself. No hesitation marks I can see, though. Suspicious death."

"Very," Bill said, looking at Wilmot.

"No prints on the knife," Rothman said. "We got that far. Prints all over everything else. Been a lot of people around recently. Looks as if — "

"He had a party last night, captain," one of the precinct detectives said. He had just come in from the foyer. He had waited. "Maybe twenty-thirty people here. Two from an apartment in the building. Name — " he checked his notebook — "name of North," he said. "Mr. and Mrs. Gerald."

"Right," Bill said. He was not surprised. Rothman raised eyebrows at him.

"You'll be in charge, lieutenant?" the assistant district attorney said. "Of your side, I mean, of course."

"Inspector O'Malley," Weigand told him. "You know that, counsellor."

"Oh," the attorney said. "Sure. Well, get us something, lieutenant."

"Captain," Mullins told him. "Captain, counsellor."

"All right, Mullins," Weigand said, but his lips twitched toward a smile. "We'll do what we can, counsellor."

The assistant district attorney went toward the door. The detective from the District Attorney's Homicide Bureau went with him.

"Sometimes," Rothman said. Bill Weigand said, "Right."

"You start with the squeal?" Rothman said. It was rhetorical — the police department started everywhere, with photographs, with fingerprints, with the patient work of a score of men, if necessary of a hundred men. It started with laboratory reports, and interviews, and searches into the past. It started everywhere. But it started also with the "squeal," which was to say the complaint, which was to say Pamela North.

The photographers were packing up. The sketch artist looked at his work, looked at the room, changed a line. He checked a measurement. The fingerprint men had worked their way into another room. All this went on without the need of direction; it had begun when Weigand, hearing Pam North's receiver cradled, had waited a moment and made the first of several calls which started the machinery. Much more would go on, now the starter had been pressed.

"Come on, sergeant," Bill Weigand said.

They went down in the elevator to the fourth floor. They went to a door which was familiar and pressed a doorbell.

"Hello, squeal," Bill Weigand said to Pamela North. "This time you found quite a body." He and Mullins went in.

IV

The strangest thing, Pamela North insisted, was that the dummy had had red hair. At that, Sergeant Mullins sighed audibly.

"All right," Pam said, in answer. "Why did it? Give me one good reason."

"Listen, Pam," Jerry said. "The hair had to be some color. Black, brown, gray, platinum blond."

"It was a male dummy," Pam said. "Not platinum. Who ever saw a dummy with red hair?"

Bill Weigand had, he said. He had seen a lot of them. Dummies in show windows, wearing the latest things in things; with red hair, sometimes with green hair.

She was not, Pam said, talking about fashion dummies in shop windows. They, of course, might have red hair — or green hair. But they were different. They were made to *look* like dummies in show windows, and to go with clothes. Whereas, this was meant to look like a man. That, she said, was the point.

"This one was meant to be somebody," she said. "Else why the red hair?" But when she

79

looked at her husband, at Bill Weigand, last of all at Mullins she saw only doubt in faces. "You don't think so?" she asked Bill.

"No," Bill said. "I think the dummy was just a gag. Intended to enliven the party."

"Then why kill it twice?" Pam asked. "Shoot it once, defenestrate it once."

"I wish," Jerry said, "you would use some other word."

"It just keeps coming out," Pam said. "It's a surprise to me, really. What — "

The bell rang, announcing someone at the door of the Norths' apartment. The man at the door was large, he looked sleepy. He said, "Excuse me, is Captain Weigand here?" and then, with Weigand produced, "Fox, sir. Eighth precinct. About this damn dummy. I talked to him" — he jerked a thumb toward the ceiling, toward the penthouse — "about it. They" — he jerked the same thumb in the same direction — "said you were the one to tell about it."

"Right," Bill said. "Go ahead, Fox."

Sergeant Fox went ahead.

"You didn't see him?" Weigand asked, when Fox had finished. "Talked to him through the door. At about two-thirty this morning?"

"Yes. I'd know his voice if I heard it again."

"He said he was Wilmot?"

"That's right, captain."

"Then you won't hear his voice again, Fox. He said the dummy had fallen off the terrace by accident?"

"Yes sir. I tried to get him to open up but — well, he sounded drunk, sir. It looks now as if I should have made him open up but — well, I didn't, captain. It didn't seem that important, nobody being hurt. Figured they could send somebody around later to get a statement and give him a summons or whatever."

It didn't matter, Weigand told him. It gave them a time. Wilmot was alive at two-thirty. He was drunk. It cleared up the question of the falling dummy.

"Mr. Fox," Pam North said, "the dummy did have red hair, didn't it?"

Fox said, "M'am?"

"Red hair," Pam said. "You saw it."

Fox looked at Weigand. Weigand nodded.

"There was a red wig in the — the debris," Fox said. "I suppose it came off the dummy." He waited. He said, "Anything else, sir?"

There wasn't, for the moment. He could go home and back to bed. He went.

"If there's a red-haired man in it somewhere," Pam said, "it would all tie together, wouldn't it?" She looked around. "Well," she said, "it might."

Without that, Bill said, they had enough. He counted on his fingers:

A young woman named Martha Evitts, who had been cruelly held up to ridicule at the party; who had reappeared that morning; who had been at least some minutes in the penthouse; who had left in excitement; who had not reported her employer's murder.

"She was terrified," Pam said. "You don't even know she was in the penthouse."

"No?" Bill said. "What terrified her, then?"

Pam thought; Pam said, "We-e-ll." They waited. "All right," Pam said, "it doesn't prove she killed him. Anyway you say he was dead by then. Long dead. Why would she go back?"

"Right," Bill said. "We don't know, of course. We'll ask."

He resumed counting.

There was the man who had dressed as a small boy. The man named Baker. He had been angry at the — joke?

The Norths thought he had. Pam was sure, further, that he was in love with Martha Evitts.

There was Wilmot's divorced wife.

"A snake in her bed," Pam said. "Didn't she say that, Jerry?"

She had.

There was Wilmot's nephew. Bill looked at Mullins, who looked at his notes. "Clyde

Parsons." He had come to a party not knowing it was a party, which had been a joke on him. What might underlie that they had yet to discover.

"He got drunk," Jerry said. "Got drunk very quickly. He's a nasty drunk, I think."

"There were a dozen others," Pam pointed out. "More than a dozen. A girl in a white dress which looked like somebody's original, and a man with a big nose — I just remember him — and the comic butler, except he probably was just hired for the occasion."

Bill shook his head at that. The butler was named Frank — Sylvester Frank. He had been, years before, a comic butler, free-lancing at parties. But for five years he had been Wilmot's butler, prankish only for Wilmot's guests.

"Wilmot wanted a monopoly, apparently," Bill said. "We've sent a man for him. Of course, there's no particular reason to suppose the murder grew out of the party."

"It must have," Pam said. "It was the kind of party it would." She considered the sentence. "Grow out of," she added, cleaning it up. "I mean — "

"Yes, Pam," Jerry told her.

"There was Mr. Monteath," Pam said, and Jerry ran the fingers of his right hand through his hair. Jerry said, "Listen, Pam." He said,

"Monteath is a second secretary or something. Maybe a first secretary. He's just come back after ten years in Europe; hadn't seen Wilmot in that long. Also, he left here last night while Wilmot was still alive. We know that."

Bill raised eyebrows. Jerry told him how they knew. Bill nodded.

"The only thing is," Pam said, "he killed the dummy. The first time, I mean." There was a long moment of silence. "Well," Pam said. "I suppose all of you are right."

The doorbell rang again. Mullins half rose; stopped and looked somewhat sheepish. "Regard this as a squad room," Jerry told him, and Mullins attended the door.

"I was told — " John Baker said, and spoke uncertainly. Dressed as a man, Pam North thought, he still looked boyish. His face was round, pink from recent shaving. His expression candid. Even if they were the same age, Pam thought, he would for years look younger than Martha Evitts, which was unfair. "I came to see whether — " Baker said doubtfully, and stopped again. "My name's Baker," he said, and this with more assurance. "I thought perhaps — "

"There might be something you could do?" Bill Weigand said. "I don't know, Mr. Baker. Is there?"

"I'm sorry," Baker said. "I don't suppose

so. Captain Weigand?"

"Right," Bill said.

"We felt at the place," Baker said. "That is, I mean Mr. Wilmot's place. The Emporium, you know?" Weigand nodded. "That someone ought to — well, to see whether there was anything we could do. To help, you know." He looked expectant, but Weigand waited. "We could hardly believe it when we heard."

"No," Bill said. "How did you hear, Mr. Baker?"

When Mr. Wilmot did not telephone the Emporium at nine-thirty, which he always did when he was not going in, and still had not called almost two hours later, someone had telephoned the apartment. Mr. Dewsnap.

Weigand repeated the name, doubt in his tone.

"Mr. Dewsnap is the manager," Baker said. "Someone — a policeman, I think — told him what had happened." He paused. "Was Mr. Wilmot really — *murdered?*" Baker said then. His tone put marks of quotation around a strange, improbable word.

"Yes," Bill said.

"You don't know by whom?' Why?"

"Not yet," Bill said.

"He was such a jolly sort of man," Baker said. "Full of fun, you know? It doesn't seem possible. It really doesn't, captain. Not to any of us."

"It seldom does, Mr. Baker," Weigand said, and Pam North said, "Won't you sit down, Mr. Baker?" He looked at her. "We met last night," Pam said. "At the party. You were dressed up as a little boy and the pretty girl with you — Miss Evans, wasn't it? — "

"Miss Evitts," Baker said.

"Of course," Pam said. "As a witch. So — " She paused. She looked at Bill Weigand, who smiled slightly with his eyes, whose eyes said, "Yes, Pam, I remembered."

"One of Mr. Wilmot's jokes," Baker said. "We — we certainly fell for it, didn't we?" He smiled, somewhat ruefully; a man remembering when he had been the butt of a famous jest. He sobered. "When you think that all the way home — to Miss Evitts's, I mean — we were laughing about it." He shook his head, noting the irony of laughter under such conditions.

"You took it so well," Pam told him. "I'm afraid most people — for example Jerry and I — " she indicated Jerry, for the record — "would have been — put out."

"Oh," Baker said, "we both know — knew — Mr. Wilmot. If you knew him, you couldn't be — put out, as you say. But — this doesn't help, does it?" The last was to Weigand.

86

"Well," Weigand said, "while we're on the subject. You and Miss Evitts left the party together? You took her home? When was that, about?"

"Why — " Baker said, and paused. He looked at Weigand for a second, his face blank. "Oh," he said. "We left, I'd say, a little after one. You were getting ready to go then, Mrs. North. Wouldn't you say a little after one?"

"Yes," Pam said.

"We found a cab and I took Martha home," Baker said. "She lives up near Columbia. It was — oh, almost two when we got there, I think. She lives with two other girls in an apartment, and I went to the door with her. Then I went home. That is, I'm living in a hotel down in the Chelsea area. Convenient to the shop, you know. I went down by subway and I got in — oh, about two-thirty. The clerk will know, because I had to pick up my key." He stopped. "Is that what you wanted to know, captain?" he said. "You don't think either of us — ?"

"We have to check on everybody," Weigand told him. "By the way — Mrs. North has told me about the masquerade costumes you and Miss Evitts wore. She got the impression that you were quite upset about it. Even angry, perhaps. You say you weren't?"

"No," Baker said. "Oh — I was embar-

87

rassed. Who wouldn't be? Perhaps I looked — upset. But that was all over in a minute."

"And Miss Evitts?"

"I told you, we laughed about it afterward."

"Mr. Wilmot had told you it was to be a costume party? And suggested what you wear?"

Baker nodded.

"He played a lot of jokes," Baker said. "Had a lot of fun." He paused. "Never a dull moment," he added, and Pam North looked at him for an instant with new intentness. But there was no change in the youthful candor of his face.

Bill Weigand nodded.

"Eventually," he said, "we'll have to dig into everything. Mr. Wilmot's business, even. Find out all we can about him. About people he knew, people who might have had something against him. About his finances. You don't know anything, offhand, about his business dealings that might be helpful?"

Baker shook his head. The Novelty Emporium couldn't, he thought, have anything to do with Mr. Wilmot's — murder. Again he used the word with disbelief.

"As I understand," Weigand said, "it's a large shop? Store? Where these — er — novelties are sold? At retail?"

Baker shook his head, slowly. It was more

than that, although it was that, too. The company sold also at wholesale. "We're jobbers, among other things." There was a manufacturing section. The company made novelties, from original designs; sold them throughout the country to retail outlets, even to other jobbers. "You'd be surprised at the size of it, actually," Baker said. "I was when I started."

Weigand nodded. He said, "By the way, when was that?"

Baker had been with the firm only about eight months. He was an auditor. He smiled. "Call it a bookkeeper," he said.

"In that job, I'd spot anything — out of the way — quick enough," he said. "I'm pretty sure you won't find anything to help you at the business end. It's all open and above-board. We'll cooperate in any way, of course but — I'm afraid you'll waste time, captain."

They were used to that, Bill told him. They wasted more time than they saved. But he appreciated Mr. Baker's opinion.

"You haven't come on anything yet, then?" John Baker said. "In his papers here or anything? Nothing to give you a lead?"

"We've just started," Bill said. "Why, Mr. Baker? You think we will?"

Baker shook his head. He said he had just

wondered. There was a pause. Baker prepared to stand.

"If there's anything at all we can do to help," he said. "All of us in the business. You'll call on us?"

"Right," Bill said.

Baker did stand up. He did not, however, leave quickly or easily; it appeared he was not one of those who can. He was naive in departure. His apologies for having been there, bothering everybody; for having intruded; for having nothing with which to help — these were numerous, a little bumbling. But he found the door, at last.

Bill Weigand sat and looked at one of the cats, and did not appear to see it. (The cat looked back, seeing Bill very clearly, possibly seeing through him.) The Norths waited for some little time. Then Bill Weigand said, "Hm-m-m" and after that, "Well."

"He *was* angry," Pam said then. "And the girl — the girl was hurt. They weren't laughing."

"No?" Bill said. "You may be right."

"I kept wondering," Pam said, "whether he wasn't — well, a little too good to be true?"

Bill Weigand half nodded. Then he stood up.

"We'd better get at it," he said. "Come on, sergeant."

They went. At the door, Bill told the Norths he would be seeing them. He spoke, it seemed to Jerry, a little absently.

The telephone rang. Pamela answered it obediently, which meant that her thoughts, too, were elsewhere. (The North who answered the telephone lost a point.) She said, "Oh yes, Mr. Monteath." She said, after a moment, "*Isn't* it?" She listened further. She said, "Why, I think that would be very nice. The Algonquin? In about half an hour?" She listened further. She said, "Thanks for calling," which was not, for her, a common locution. She replaced the telephone.

"It's on the radio," she said. "Mr. Monteath wants us to have lunch with him. I said we would. All right?"

"I guess so," Jerry said. "Why?"

Pam shrugged slightly. She said Mr. Monteath hadn't said.

"Maybe," Pam said, "he just thinks we're nice people to have lunch with. Do you suppose that's it?"

"I wouldn't know," Jerry told her.

She nodded.

"Were you a very close friend of his?" she asked. "Ten years ago, or whenever it was?"

Jerry shook his head. They had played tennis together a few times, had drinks together. "You met him," Jerry said.

"Once," Pam said. "Perhaps twice. He seems to appreciate us more now, doesn't he? Do you suppose murder draws people together?"

Less went on in the penthouse apartment. The body was no longer there; most of the blood was gone from the floor, but in the interstices between the tiles blood darkness remained. Rothman had gone, and the photographers, and the print men. The precinct was gone, except for two uniformed men. The detectives from the First District remained; Sergeant Stein from the Homicide Squad had appeared. He had what there was.

Item, Sylvester Frank, the butler, was not immediately to be found. But — he had been there that morning. The routine check among tenants on the floor below the penthouse, undertaken without great expectations, had been unexpectedly productive. A woman, reaching out to pick up a newspaper in front of her door, had seen Frank climbing the stairs to the penthouse, as she had seen him on many other mornings. He had looked as he looked on any morning. (Told how this morning had differed from other mornings, she had gasped, turned white.)

"Frank doesn't live in," Stein said. "This place is mostly living room; two bedrooms, two baths, kitchen, no servant's room. Apparently Frank left after the party last night, went home — he's got a room on the west side — came back at the usual time. Then, disappeared."

"Fire stairs," Bill said. "I wonder why?"

Stein could only shrug.

Item, Martha Evitts, who had been taken up had stayed briefly, had been taken down again — "She looked as if she'd seen a dozen ghosts, the elevator man says" — was also not to be found. She had not gone to her office. She had not gone to her apartment uptown. She was being sought, as was Frank.

"If she found the body, she didn't call," Stein said. "We've checked that. Secretive of her."

"Right," Bill said. "Non-cooperative."

Item, the knife had been Wilmot's, one of a set designed for various uses in a kitchen, kept in a slotted box on a counter in the kitchen. It was, in length, somewhere between a paring knife and a carving knife. It had a tapering blade and a sharp point; it was a good knife.

"No trick?" Bill asked, and Stein shook his head. He went to a table and brought the knife and Bill looked at it, finding no trick — finding it English made, hollow ground, a useful knife for a variety of purposes. A set of such knives

93

would, Bill thought, appeal to a man who liked good tools, who was handy with them — who, by extension, might like contrivances. Bill guessed that the kitchen held many useful gadgets, said so, was told it did. That fitted Wilmot well enough, but that was no longer the point. It had not been Wilmot who was handy with his knife.

Weigand looked around the penthouse, with Stein as guide. The foyer, the big, oblong living room with glass and glass doors on three sides, the two small bedrooms and the two compact baths; the neat laboratory of a kitchen, with an electric oven built into one wall, electric surface units and a refrigerator combined; a garbage disposal unit built into a sink, a dishwasher, full of glasses — all very efficient, all a little "gadgety." That fitted, also.

They went out to the terrace, which went around three sides of the penthouse. It was some fifteen feet wide at its widest, which was on the side of the building overlooking the street; narrower on the two other sides. French doors opened on it from all rooms except the baths. The penthouse area comprised only a part of the roof; the remainder, separated from the terrace by a low wall, was merely roof. There was a housing for the elevator machinery and in that there was a small door. Bill looked in. A steel ladder ran down one side of a narrow well, which held steel cables. Presumably, if one went down the ladder, one would find some exit below.

There was another door, this one into a narrow, sloped-roof shed. Bill opened it. Steep metal stairs ran down to another door — a fire door. This was the topmost entrance to fire stairs, which would, at the bottom, give on the street or on a court from which the street could easily be reached. Sylvester Frank could have used this exit from the roof after his morning visit. As easily, he could have got to the floor below through the foyer and, there, found another door to the fire stairs. Either the ladder through the elevator housing or the fire stairs might provide access to the roof, as well as exit from it. Fire doors can usually be opened from one side — be opened toward escape. Bill looked again at the fire door on the roof. It had knobs on both sides, could be opened by a person standing inside, on the narrow stairs. The roof was, therefore, available to anyone who got himself into the building, which was no chore at all. Mr. Wilmot might easily have entertained the marauder he had, for party purposes, simulated. Well, people had to be able, somehow, to get to the roof of a building. Roofs sprang leaks, for one thing.

They went back into the penthouse itself.

"I don't suppose," Bill said, "that Wilmot was thoughtful enough to make a list of his party guests?"

If he had been, they hadn't found it. There was a desk at one end of the living room; beside it there was a three-drawer filing case, inconspicuously built in. In the wall above the desk, conventionally behind a picture, there was a wall safe. The filing case had been opened; the safe, as yet, had not. A man was on his way for that. Two detectives were going over papers from the filing case, one seated at the desk, with papers piled in front of him; the other, less comfortably, on his knees in front of the case. Weigand walked to them; his eyebrows enquired.

"Nope," the man at the desk said. "Nothing that sticks out. Business stuff, mostly. A wad of drawings of machinery or something."

"Novelties, probably," Bill said.

"Could be," the detective said, and went on with it.

"Where," the uniformed man in the foyer said, loudly, "do you think you're going, mister?"

" — be damned," a slurred voice said. "Had it right, did they? Somebody really got the old buzzard? Old Uncle Buzzard?"

Bill Weigand moved across the living room

96

quickly. He stood at the door to the foyer.

A tall, thin young man in a gray suit — a white-faced young man, with disordered black hair — stood facing a policeman. The young man swayed slightly as he stood. He looked as if he might have slept in his gray suit.

"Old Uncle Buzzard," the young man said, and it was evident he was drunk. He turned to Weigand, then. "Whata you want?" he said. The policeman looked at Bill Weigand; Weigand shook his head, briefly.

"Mr. Wilmot was your uncle?" Bill asked, and got "Tha's right, who're you?"

Bill told him.

"Policeman," the young man said. He looked at Bill. "Don' look it," he said. He swayed further. "Next of kin," he said. "Pay respects." He sought to pull himself together. "Clyde Parsons," he said, and gestured toward himself.

"Come in," Bill said, and indicated the policeman's task. The policeman took Clyde Parsons by the arm. He was shaken off. "Think I can't walk?" Parsons said. "Think I'm drunk?"

Bill's gesture gave instructions. The uniformed man released Parsons, who could walk, if not steadily. He walked into the living room, he sat down, sprawling a little, in a deep chair. Momentarily, he put both hands to his head. Then he put them on the arms of the chair.

"Little dizzy for a minute," he said, and his voice, while still blurred, was steadier. He looked up at Bill Weigand. "All right, I'm drunk," he said. "So what? Right to be drunk, haven't I?"

"If you like," Bill said.

"Anyway, he started me off," Parsons said. "You hear about that?"

"No," Bill said. "Why don't you tell me?"

"Don't know whether it's any of your business, come to think of it," Parsons said. "Just came around to see whether they had it right. Somebody kill the old boy?"

"Yes," Bill said. "Somebody did, Mr. Parsons. Somebody killed your uncle."

"Anybody who knew him," Parsons said. "Anybody at all. Could have done it myself." He paused. He put his hands to his head again. "Didn't, though," he said. "No use saying I did."

Briefly, Bill considered Clyde Parsons. There was no point in a statement; it wouldn't stick. Mullins loomed near and raised eyebrows, indicated his notebook. Bill shook his head. But still —

"You were here last night?" Bill said. "At the party your uncle gave?" He paused. Parsons was looking around the room. "Want some coffee?" Bill asked him.

"Want to sober me up, don't you?" Parsons said. "Everybody wants to sober the poor guy up. Nobody ever does. Alcoholics Anonish — Anonymous. Everybody. 'Cept old Uncle Buzzard. He thought it was funny." He considered. "Funny as hell," he said. His drawn white face was not funny; his tormented dark eyes were not funny. "Six months I went," he said. "Got the poor damned fool on the wagon, they figured. Forgot good old uncle." He paused again. "Know what happened?" he said.

"Tell me."

"Said he was sick," Parsons said. "Had an attack. Wanted to see me. Make everything up."

"When was this?"

It had been late the afternoon before. Frank had telephoned Parsons at six or thereabouts. "Back from the office," Clyde Parsons said. "Had a job yesterday. Hell with it." Frank had said that Byron Wilmont had been suddenly taken ill — very ill. They were afraid it was a heart attack. He wanted to see his nephew that evening, but not immediately. The doctor was with Wilmot then, Frank said. They would know more at ten o'clock, or thereabouts. Parsons was to come then.

"Hadn't seen him for months," Parsons said. "We had a blowup — when was it? Early last fall. Said I was a drunken bum and needn't expect anything from him. I said he was an objectionable old fool, or something like that." Parsons paused. "Could be we were both right," he said.

But now, Frank had told him, Wilmot, suddenly very ill, had had a change of heart. He wanted to see his only kinsman, wanted "to make things right."

"How, did you think?" Bill asked the white-faced man.

"What do you think?" Parsons asked him. "The old boy had a lot of money. Last time I saw him he was going to make a will and leave the whole business to charity. Charity, for God's sake! Leave out his only relative — me. I told him what he could do with it."

"You meant it?"

"Then, sure. But — well, who wants to have a fight with a lot of money? If he'd decided blood thicksher — thicker than water, s'all right with me." He paused again and looked around the room. "Mother's brother anyway," he said. "Old fool, but still — " He looked at Weigand. "Things get mixed up," he said. "Not just one reason. Know that?"

"Yes," Bill said. "You came here. At about ten?"

100

"Sometime around then, little later, maybe. Found this party going on. Everybody singing and dancing. The old — Uncle Byron laughing his head off. Saying he knew I'd come running if I got the idea he might — Well, there it was. Joke on me. Thrown in with a lot of people I didn't know, looking like — like a poor relation. So he says, 'Stay for the party. May as well get what you can.' Then he has Frank bring me a drink. Putting it up to me — like saying, 'You poor sap. Can't take a drink like everybody else, can you?' So — I took the drink."

"And went on."

"Whata you think? Sure I went on. He knew I would. Six months without it. On a job three months so — phooey! Funny, wasn't it?"

"Why?" Bill asked. "What was the point of it?"

"Made a fool of me," Parsons said. "What do you want? What did he want? Make fools of people." He seemed to grow abruptly more sober. "He made a career of that," Parsons said. "Don't you realize that, captain? Maybe a psychiatrist could tell you why. He started on me when I was a kid." He paused again. "Maybe I didn't laugh hard enough," he said. "He liked people to laugh when they — oh, tripped over a wire and fell in a lake. Used to call me — what was it? — 'that sullen brat.'

When I wanted to get in the — " He stopped. "Skip it," he said.

"Specifically," Bill said, "you thought he wanted you to come and make things up? You gathered he was going to change his will?"

"All right," Parsons said. "Something like that. Make a will, I guess. Anyway, last fall I got the idea he hadn't made one. Maybe he did later. I don't know."

"You didn't learn last night?"

"When I start to drink," Parsons said, "it hits me fast. A couple, and I've had it. Don't remember all he said. Don't — well, there's a lot of things about last night I don't remember."

"When you came in," Bill said, "you said something about being next of kin. You are?"

"Yes."

Weigand waited for the thin young man to pick it up. When he did not, Weigand said, "Meaning, if there's no will you'd inherit?"

"Could be," Parsons said. "Is there a will?"

"I don't know, Mr. Parsons," Weigand said. "It may be in his safe. We haven't opened that yet. It may be at his lawyer's. Perhaps, as you think, there isn't a will."

Parsons said, "Yeah." He did not seem greatly interested. He said, "The radio said he was stabbed. That right?"

"Right," Bill said. "When did you leave here last night, Mr. Parsons? Or was it this morning?"

"Leave?" Parsons said. "Oh. I don't know. Aunt Trudie can tell you. I went when she did. She wanted me to go home with her. Wanted to sober me up. Everybody wants to sober me up."

"You went with her?"

"Not me," Parsons said. "Went looking for a bar, I guess. Seem to have found one." He closed his eyes. He looked ill. "Found several, probably," he said. "I don't remember. When I get to drinking, I don't, usually." He opened his eyes. "Remember going down from here," he said. "Something about a taxicab. Aunt Trudie wanted me to get in, and I didn't. Don't think I did. Then I was home — maybe it was an hour ago — and turned on the radio and heard about — this."

"That's all you remember?"

"That's all. You think I came back and killed Uncle Buzzard?"

"I don't know," Weigand said. "Did you?"

"Don't know either," Parsons said. He seemed momentarily more cheerful. "Might have seemed like a good idea. But, on the other hand, I was probably pretty drunk. Probably he'd just have pushed me and I'd have fallen down. Anyway, they say I don't usually get that nasty when I'm drunk. Never knifed anybody I know of."

He leaned forward a little in the chair, clutching the chair arms.

"Not very satisfactory, is it?" he said.

"Not very," Bill Weigand said. "You know of anybody who might have wanted your uncle dead?"

"Anybody who knew him, I'd think," Parsons said. (Parsons was, Bill thought, sobering rather rapidly, which was interesting.) "Specifically, no, I don't. If Aunt Trudie wanted to kill him — but she wouldn't kill anybody — she'd have done it years ago. Used to put snakes in her bed, just for a laugh."

"Actually?"

"He did once. Four or five years ago. She didn't like it. Went to Reno."

"But was here last night?"

"Seems to have been. Sure — she was." He paused. "I don't know why," he said. "Ask her."

"Right," Bill said. "We will. You were here when there was this — incident of the dummy?"

"Sure. Anyway, I was partly here. I didn't — well, I didn't pay much attention. Lot of banging and people yelling. Knew it was one of uncle's gags. Usually, there was one big

104

gag — one real knock-'em-dead thing."

"The dummy had red hair," Weigand said, and was surprised to hear himself saying, "Does that mean anything to you?"

"Mean anything? What'd it mean?"

"I don't know," Bill said. "Nothing, probably. Later, the dummy fell off the terrace. Landed on the sidewalk. Fell off accidentally, your uncle said."

Parsons said he knew nothing about that. He said that it would be his guess his uncle pushed it off. For a gag.

"Possibly," Bill said. "You know a man with red hair?"

"What the hell?" Parsons said. "Probably known half a dozen."

"Connected with your uncle in any way?"

Parsons appeared to consider. Absently, he took a pipe from his jacket pocket, looked at it, put it back. In the end he shook his head. "If you're thinking about the dummy, it was just a gag," he said. "You wouldn't wonder about it if you'd known my uncle."

"Probably not," Bill said. "You haven't any ideas, Mr. Parsons? Any that will help us?"

Parsons shook his head. But then he hesitated. He said, "No," but dragged the word. Then he leaned forward again.

"I had a feeling he was up to something," Parsons said. "Don't know what."

"Your uncle? What do you mean, Mr. Parsons?"

"I don't know," Parsons said. "I got to feeling that way last summer. Before we had this — disagreement. Felt he was up to — something. I don't know why. It was just a feeling I got. Doesn't help much, does it?"

"It's vague, certainly," Weigand said. "You mean — in business? In his personal life? What do you mean?"

"You know," Parsons said, "I'm damned if I know. Probably something I just made up. Maybe he'd just thought of a new line of gadgets. Maybe — I tell you I don't know. Don't even remember what got me started thinking that."

"Try to," Bill told him, and it seemed, for a minute or more, that Parsons did try. But he ended by shaking his head. Then, uncertainly, he stood up. For a moment, standing, he swayed. He smiled faintly, uncomfortably.

"All right if I go?" he said.

"Right," Bill told him. "Go home and get some sleep."

Parsons said, "Sure." He pulled his tie straight; he brushed ineffectually at his suit jacket. He said, again, "Sure." He went. He was not, Bill thought, going to sleep. He was going to the nearest bar.

"The safe man's here," Mullins said. "He

tell you anything?"

"Parsons?" Bill said. "I don't know, sergeant. Probably he's Wilmot's heir if Wilmot didn't make a will. Parsons thinks he didn't."

Mullins said, "Hm-m." He said, "He's working on it."

They walked to the end of the room and watched the safe man work on the safe. He got it open, without too much trouble.

There was nothing in it but money. There was a little under thirty thousand dollars in fifty and twenty dollar bills, none of which was new. It took them a time to count it, but that was what it came to — twenty-eight thousand, seven hundred and fifty dollars. It appeared that Mr. Wilmot had not wanted to run out of cash.

V

Thursday, 1:30 P.M. *to* 3:20 P.M.

Arthur Monteath sat on a sofa, against a wall, in a corner of the Algonquin's lobby. Pam and Jerry North saw him before they were themselves seen; Mr. Monteath looked, waiting, precisely as Pam had always sought to look herself — not like a person waiting, not perched; observant but relaxed. He did better at it than she ever had, she thought, preparing a smile as she walked toward Mr. Monteath, with Jerry behind her. Monteath looked up; Pam smiled. Monteath rose, without struggle, although the sofa was deeply cushioned. He stood awaiting them and did not put hands in pockets. She must remind Jerry of that, Pam thought, and wondered whether Mr. Monteath had sat with his back to a wall because of senators. After all, Pam thought, he's State Department, and held out a slim hand, which was taken, just perceptibly bowed over.

They sat, after greetings. Monteath tapped the plunger of the little bell on the table and, across the lobby, a white-jacketed waiter heard at once and came toward them. Waiters, even at the Algonquin, did not always hear at once. Perhaps it was, Pam thought, a tribute to Mr. Monteath's tailoring. Even now, as he sat again, Mr. Monteath's gray suit jacket did not bunch at the back of the neck. Pam looked quickly at Jerry's jacket. Probably, she thought, it's the way people sit. She said, "A very dry martini, with lemon peel, please. No olive, please. Just a twist of lemon peel." "A martini," the waiter said. "Without an olive," Pam said.

"We knew a woman once," Pam said, "who put olives in all the glasses and then poured the liquid in the bottle — the stuff olives live in, you know — into the shaker with the martinis. Ugh!"

"Ugh!" Mr. Monteath said, politely. He offered Pamela, then Jerry, cigarettes from a leather case. He told them it had been pleasant running into them again. He said he had spoken to the maître d' about a table. He said that, walking to the Algonquin, it had felt like spring. He said it was pleasant to be again in New York, even if briefly. He said, "Ah," when the drinks came, and raised his and smiled over it and said, "Cheers." He said, "Get much tennis these days?" to Jerry, who said he didn't. Monteath said he had passed where the Park Avenue courts had been and there was an apartment house there now and sighed briefly.

"Somehow," Jerry said, "I always turned up on the court without any back run. Remember?"

Monteath did. He remembered the pro at the courts, who could, and sometimes did, play with a racket in either hand. Jerry also remembered him. Well, Pam thought, sipping her drink, they're better than golfers, but not much. Mr. Monteath had got in a little tennis in the south of France the previous autumn. Jerry hadn't played since last September. "No overhead at all, any more," Jerry said. Arthur Monteath hadn't either. "Overhead goes first, of course," he said, and the two nodded agreement to that. Pamela smiled a little fixedly, and continued to sip. She had, she was forced to admit, expected more. "What," Mr. Monteath enquired, "ever happened to Harry? Harry Cunningham. Remember him?"

Jerry did.

"Isn't it," Pam heard herself saying, "terrible what happened to Mr. Wilmot?"

It sounded a little gauche. She felt that Mr. Monteath must be wincing, although there was no outward evidence of this. Well, Pam thought, there's no use letting somebody set the pace if they won't.

"A shocking thing," Monteath said, and both he and Jerry looked at her, and waited.

"Right after we were all there," Pam said. "And — " She paused, because there was suddenly a picture in her mind. "I'm afraid I'll never forget the way he looked," she said, and then knew, coldly, that she never would. She put her glass down and, as he saw her face, Jerry reached out to touch her hand, to hold it, for a moment, under his.

"My dear!" Monteath said. "I hadn't realized."

Pam nodded.

"I did," she said. "The elevator man and I. Of course, Miss Evitts first but she — well, she didn't do anything. So we — we had to. I made the squeal, really."

"Squeal?" Monteath said. There was blank astonishment in his voice, diplomacy having slipped.

"Called the police," Jerry said. "She's just heard the — er — term. From a friend of ours who's a detective."

"Oh, yes," Monteath said. "I've heard something about you and him, haven't I? A chap named — Weygand?"

"Weigand," Pam said. "Bill Weigand. Had you?"

Monteath nodded. He did not amplify. Well, Pam thought, it's not a secret, of course. But still, he's been away. Even if we do get in the newspapers a little, sometimes, you wouldn't think . . .

"This friend of yours," Monteath said. "He's a Homicide man, isn't he? Probably be in on this?"

"Oh yes," Pam said. "He is. He's there now, probably. Or — or somewhere talking to people." She paused for a moment. "People who were at the party," she added. And she found she was watching Monteath's face.

But she could read nothing in it. He nodded slowly. Then he looked at their glasses, reached a hand toward the little bell. But Raul came out of the Oak Room before he touched it, found them and came to the corner. He greeted the Norths, told Monteath that their table was ready. At the table, Monteath ordered more drinks. "The perfects?" Raul asked, and Jerry nodded. "Wonderful martinis," Pam promised. "Much better than outside. Unless they send them outside from inside, of course."

Monteath looked at her. He nodded again, this time doubtfully.

"About Wilmot," he said then. "I don't suppose your friend will have much difficulty finding out who was there?"

"Hardly any," Pam said. "People will remember other people, of course. We told him about Miss Evitts and Mr. Baker. And that you were there, Mr. Monteath."

"Of course," Monteath said. "I assumed you had, actually." He looked at Pam. Now he smiled. "I'll admit I wondered," he said. "I realized it couldn't be helped. Still — " He shrugged. "Won't make me popular in the department," he said.

They waited.

"Mine's a queer job," he said. "We're supposed to avoid — er — unfavorable associations." He smiled faintly. "Almost any association can be that," he said. "And a man like Wilmot — " He ended with`another shrug.

"You mean," Pam said, "because he got himself killed?"

Monteath hesitated. He said, "Of course, that too." But he did not amplify. The drinks came. They ordered food.

"Nobody can blame you just because you went to a party and afterward somebody killed your host," Pam said. "I mean, you can't just not ever go anywhere. And how can anybody tell beforehand?"

"She means — " Jerry began, but Monteath smiled and shook his head slightly. He said it was perfectly clear what Mrs. North meant, and that her point was well taken. He hoped the department would be equally — observant. Nevertheless, a high value was placed on discretion.

"Will it matter much?" Jerry asked and was told that, probably, it wouldn't.

"They'll wish it hadn't happened," Monteath said. "So do I. But —it did." He considered his drink. "Your police friend will want to see me, I suppose," he said. "As a matter of routine?"

"I'd think so," Pam said, and Jerry nodded his head.

"I don't suppose you know whether he's got any — leads?" Monteath asked. "Probably hasn't. Yet anyway."

"No," Jerry said, "I shouldn't think so."

"He was stabbed, according to what I heard on the radio," Monteath said. "Was that right?"

Pam told him it was; told him something of what she had seen from the doorway to the big living room. She told him, too, why she had gone to the penthouse — something of the blank fear, or shock, in the eyes of Martha Evitts.

"Of course," she said, "there was the business about the dummy first. You remember the dummy? The mannequin?"

"Oh yes," Monteath said. "I remember the dummy, Mrs. North. Very — unpleasantly. I thought for a moment there — well, what Wilmot wanted me to think. That I'd killed a man."

"It was a damn fool thing," Jerry said.

"I thought so," Monteath said. "Of course, I was a little — well, call it prejudiced. Probably seemed very funny to Wilmot."

"He must have been a strange sort of person," Pam said, and paused while the waiter delivered, to her, corned beef and cabbage. "My," Pam said, "I must have been hungry." The waiter left broiled sea bass with Jerry, eggs benedict with Arthur Monteath. The waiter withdrew. "A very strange sort of person," Pam said. "To go to so much trouble for — well, it wasn't particularly funny, or anything, was it?"

Monteath shook his head.

"Unless it meant something more," Pam said. "I keep wondering about the red hair."

"Yes," Jerry said. "You do, don't you?"

"Well," Pam said, turning to him. "Why the red hair, then?"

"I don't know, dear," Jerry said. "I'm very sorry, but I don't know." Monteath looked from one of them to the other. "The mannequin had red hair," Jerry told him, and Monteath's face cleared. He said that, now, he remembered.

"Well," Pam said, "it fell out, or off. A while after you'd gone, it went by our window. I thought it was Mr. Wilmot, at first."

"Fell off?" Monteath repeated.

They told him what they knew. He shook his head. He said, after a pause, that Wilmot must have been drunk.

"I suppose so," Pam said. "The sergeant said he was. Only — he didn't seem drunk when we all left, did he?"

"He'd been drinking," Monteath said. "Perhaps he had another one or two after everybody'd gone and they caught up with him. I've known it to happen."

"Yes," Pam said. "Speaking of people being drunk. Wasn't it too bad — I mean, wasn't it unpleasant — about Mr. Wilmot's nephew? You said you knew him, Mr. Monteath."

"No," Monteath said. "I said I'd heard of him. He wanted to get into the department — career service. He'd more or less trained for it. He got turned down."

"Why?"

Monteath shrugged well-tailored shoulders. (Even so, his jacket did not wrinkle at the collar. It was almost exasperating.) Monteath said he didn't know. He said that, when they decided a man wasn't cut out for the work, they could find a hundred reasons.

"Perhaps he went with the wrong crowd in kindergarten," Jerry suggested. Monteath smiled faintly. He said that, nowadays, almost anything was possible.

"Perhaps," Pam said, "he drank too much."

"Perhaps," Monteath said. "I really don't know, Mrs. North. Because I knew, or had known, his uncle, I was asked about Parsons. Said he was all right, as far as I knew. Heard later he didn't make it. Remembered about it when I saw him last night." He paused. "Obviously, if he drank too much, they wouldn't consider him the type," he added. "Possibly, on the other hand, he merely failed the physical."

They ate for a time in silence. There was really, Pam discovered, a great deal of corned beef.

"How long do these things take, usually?" Monteath asked then.

"These things?" Jerry repeated and then said, "Oh, you mean Bill's investigations?"

Monteath nodded.

"Anywhere from — oh, a day to a year," Jerry said. "Or longer. They don't close the files on murder. There's no way of telling."

"I've got to get on to Washington," Monteath said. "As a matter of fact — well, I've got a new assignment coming up, probably. I wondered how long — "

"Oh," Pam said. "Not very, I'm sure. It's just routine for you, of course. Hardly even that. But — we'll tell Bill, if you like. I'm sure he won't want to hold you up."

It wasn't really important, Monteath told

them. Not a matter of hours, at any rate. He had merely wondered.

"In any case," he said, "I promised to do something about the old boy's book. Speaking of the book — "

He spoke of the book; afterward of other things.

It was almost forty-five minutes later that Arthur Monteath looked at the watch on his wrist and seemed surprised. It was later than he thought. Unfortunately, he had an appointment. If they would forgive him?

They would. Jerry, as a matter of fact, had to get back to his office. They rose together. Outside the hotel, Monteath would drop them. But he was going uptown. They must take the first cab to answer the doorman's whistle. But it was he who had the appointment, was late for it. He acquiesced, and the doorman's whistle shrilled. The doorman stood in the middle of Forty-fourth Street and whistled and made gestures. A cab checked itself, swung in. The Norths would not reconsider; it would be only a matter of minutes. They would see Mr. Monteath again before he left for Washington.

Monteath got into the cab, said, "Waldorf," to the driver. The cab pulled from the curb, the doorman resumed his shrilling. Monteath's cab went east in Forty-fourth.

And, from the parking garage across Forty-fourth Street, a nondescript sedan pulled out. It fell in behind the cab, crept after it; stopped behind it when, far ahead, the column was halted by red lights at Fifth Avenue.

"For heaven's sake!" Pam North said. "Look who it is!"

Jerry said, "What?"

"In the car," Pam said. "Behind Mr. Monteath's cab."

Jerry looked; Jerry shook his head. So far as he was concerned, the car held the blur of a man. The left ear, to be sure, was discernible. It was not, however, identifying. Jerry said, "Nope."

"Mr. Baker," Pam said. "Of all people. *Following Mr. Monteath!*"

"Listen, Pam," Jerry said.

But Pamela North was positive. Jerry knew she never forgot faces. (To this Jerry did not directly respond.) Anyway, she had had a good look. The sedan contained Baker — John Baker, the man in rompers, the employee of the late Mr. Wilmot, the co-victim with Martha Evitts of Mr. Wilmot's humor. He was following Arthur Monteath. He had, moreover, been waiting to follow Mr. Monteath.

Gerald North used the word "fortuitous," but he used it without confidence. It would be unfair to Pam North to say that, at that, she snorted. She was not constructed to snort. But she made a sound.

"If we could only get a cab," Pam said, and joined the doorman in waving. But it was some minutes before they were in a cab, and by then it was useful for transportation, but not pursuit. It took them toward Jerry's office.

"We'll have to tell Bill, of course," Pam said. "I'll call him when I get home."

"You're sure it was Baker?"

She was. Then she should call.

"But there's more, isn't there?" Pam said. "Why the lunch? Not to talk about tennis. Not even to talk about the ambassador's book. You saw that?"

Jerry had wondered. He admitted that.

"He'd found out we knew Bill. Figured we'd know what was going on. Why?"

"Possibly," Jerry said. "You're guessing, Pam. As to why — he wants to get away, to Washington. Wants as much as he can to avoid notoriety. Thinks we might help."

"Um-m-m," Pamela North said. "I suppose so." She was silent for a block. "You know what we forgot?" she said, then. "We forgot to ask him if he knows a man with red hair."

"Listen, Pam," Jerry said. "Everybody knows at least — " The cab stopped. "Keep your flag down," Jerry told the driver. "The lady'll keep the cab."

120

The lady did, and went home in it. But, when she telephoned, Acting Captain William Weigand was not available. Nor was Sergeant Mullins.

"Never when you want them," Pam told Martini, who answered briskly, if not directly to the point.

They had the contents of the late Mr. Wilmot's filing cabinet, and it was not clear that it got them anywhere in particular. It appeared that Mr. Wilmot's home had been to some extent a second office — most of the filed correspondence had to do with the business of the Novelty Emporium. It had to do with orders for Mr. Wilmot's somewhat peculiar merchandise, with offers of merchandise suitably novel, with orders for the raw material of such merchandise. There were carbons of several letters in German and three in French.

They had the "wad" of drawings, which was actually an orderly enough sheaf of blueprints. The drawings appeared to be designs of — well, "gadgets" was the word which jumped to the mind, and lodged there. Technical men no doubt would come up with something more precise, given time. They would be given time.

They had twenty-eight thousand, seven

hundred and fifty dollars in bills of various denominations. It was, Sergeant Mullins remarked, a nice round sum. It was also a considerable sum to find in anyone's wall safe. It was of especial interest to find it in the safe of a man who had just been murdered.

Which of course did not, Acting Captain William Weigand reminded himself, as he drove his Buick into the tunnel to Queens, mean that the contents of Byron Wilmot's safe had necessary connection with the fact of Byron Wilmot's murder. The simple fact was that, when a man was murdered, everything about him became, for the time being, of especial interest. The interest was, at first, distributed — spread thin. That Mr. Wilmot had written letters in German to, apparently, a manufacturing company in West Germany might prove as interesting as the fact that he had died with twenty-eight thousand, seven hundred and fifty dollars in his wall safe. It was true that, from a quick glance by a man who knew German only moderately, the letters were concerned with arrangements to have manufactured in Germany certain articles which Wilmot had proposed to sell in the United States. Unless Wilmot had been killed by a rival manufacturer, one who carried free competition somewhat to extremes —

"Of course," Sergeant Mullins said, from

his seat beside Weigand, "it could be payoff money."

It could, Bill Weigand agreed, coming out of the tunnel to Long Island. It could also be a sum kept available to satisfy demands for compensation by those joked against. It could be, merely, money that Byron Wilmot had kept around so that he wouldn't run short over weekends.

"O.K., Loot," Mullins said. "So we don't know."

"Payoff for what?" Weigand asked, going around a truck.

"Maybe he had a lot of guys working for him," Mullins suggested. "Maybe he handled hot stuff. Maybe he was a bookie."

There was no end to the possibilities. Weigand agreed to that. At this stage, there seldom was — particularly in the screwy ones.

"Jeeze," Mullins said. "This sure is. Dummies falling off roofs, men in rompers, women screaming on phonographs. *And* the Norths."

He was beginning, Bill told him, to think like Deputy Chief Inspector Artemus O'Malley. It was a tendency to be discouraged. So far, at any rate, the Norths had merely gone to a party.

"And found a body," Mullins said.

"One thing leads to another," Bill told him, and drove toward Forest Hills, toward the

123

home of Mrs. Gertrude Wilmot, former wife of Byron Wilmot and one of a good many people to be seen. At the moment, a person to start with.

Mrs. Wilmot lived in a comfortable house in a row of comfortable houses on a pleasant street which would, by June, lie in the shade cast by great maple trees. They walked up to the house along a cement walk, hedged by pruned hemlocks. Mrs. Wilmot herself came to the door when they rang the bell.

All over the country, Bill Weigand thought, such pleasant women in their middle years come to the doors of such houses when bells are pressed. They look up, ready to smile, at men who may be friends of friends, who may be selling brushes or vacuum cleaners. They look down, smiling already, on small boys collecting for newspaper deliveries, offering to mow lawns. They speak with a variety of regional accents, their clothes are different in cut and color. They are pleasant women, not easily perturbed.

Mrs. Wilmot seemed unperturbed. She looked up at Bill Weigand and smiled and said, "Yes?" in a voice without perturbation — and with not much expectation, either — and looked only a little puzzled when Weigand introduced himself. She had not, it appeared, been listening to radio news.

A voice came through the opened door, from a living room. "In a moderate oven," the voice said, with cadenced enthusiasm. Not, at any rate, to radio news of murder.

"I'm afraid I have bad news for you, Mrs. Wilmot," Weigand said, and then her round, rather pretty, face did change. Her eyes widened and anxiety showed.

She said, "Not Clyde? Something's happened to — " Her voice was thin. She stopped because Bill Weigand shook his head.

"No," he said, "not Mr. Parsons. We'd better come in, Mrs. Wilmot."

She stepped back. They went through a small entrance hall into a living room of chintz. On a television screen a young woman in an afternoon dress, with a frill of apron, bent to remove something from an oven, no doubt moderate. She murmured of golden browns; faded into nothing as Mrs. Wilmot turned a knob.

Mrs. Wilmot turned to face them. She was of medium height, rounded comfortably, but only plump. Her gray hair had been arranged by accomplished fingers. She had blue eyes, and they were wide as she waited.

"It's about Mr. Wilmot," Weigand said. "I'm sorry to have to tell you — "

But she interrupted.

125

"Byron," she said. "Oh."

It was as if she had come upon an anticlimax. It was then as if she caught herself. The expression of anxiety did not return to her face, but it reflected what might be regarded as concern.

"Oh," she said, "I do hope nothing — "

"I'm sorry," Bill said. "Mr. Wilmot was found dead this morning. In his apartment. I'm afraid someone killed him, Mrs. Wilmot."

She said, "Oh! How dreadful!" She said, "How really dreadful!" She sat in a chintz-covered chair, and motioned to other chairs gay in chintz.

Bill Weigand re-expressed regret at the news he brought. She nodded her head as he spoke. She said, then, that it was a shock, of course. But then she straightened.

"I won't pretend," she said. "It's just a — a shock. You don't have to be upset, captain. We weren't — we hadn't been together for several years, you know. I'm terribly distressed that such a dreadful thing should have happened — that poor Byron — " She finished with a small movement of well-shaped hands. Then she said, "But — " and let the conjunction suffice.

It made things easier.

"We have to try to find out what happened," Bill told her. "Your former husband was murdered. We have to find out why, by whom."

"Of course," she said. "But I don't know. I hardly knew anything about him in the last few years." She paused. "Perhaps I never did," she said. "He was a strange man. A strange and — " She stopped. She seemed to consider. "We shouldn't speak ill of the dead," she said. "Particularly, I shouldn't. I was his wife." She paused again. "Actually," she said, "I'm not really so much surprised that somebody — killed him. He was a cruel man." She nodded her head. "A very cruel man," she said.

"Cruel?" Bill said. "How, Mrs. Wilmot?"

"Every way," she said. "Those dreadful — he called them jokes. But always they hurt people. I know, captain. Take what he did to Clyde — " She stopped abruptly. "But Clyde wouldn't hurt anybody," she said then, quickly. "Anybody but himself." She paused for a moment. "Clyde's my husband's nephew," she said.

"I know," Bill said. "I've talked to Mr. Parsons. He told me about Mr. Wilmot's little — joke on him last night."

"A malicious thing," Mrs. Wilmot said. "Byron did so many things like that. But Clyde wouldn't — "

"I haven't suggested Mr. Parsons did anything," Bill told her.

"Never," she said. "He never would. But — but Byron was cruel to so many people. Those poor young people last night. The awful thing he did to poor Arthur."

"Monteath," Bill said, and she nodded.

"Making him think it had happened again," she said. "Think how — how awful that would be for anyone. And there were — oh so many other people. So many people must have hated Byron." She looked up. "Sometimes I hated him," she said. "I didn't kill him, though."

"Yes," Bill said. "Tell me about last night, Mrs. Wilmot. What you remember."

She told him. She had remembered a good deal, little of it he had not already heard from the Norths. Her interest, he felt, had been centered on her nephew. There was anger against Wilmot when she spoke of Clyde Parsons. "Always he did that," she said. "Played on Clyde's weakness. I know it's a weakness. Everybody does. Everybody else has tried to help. But Byron — it wasn't the first time. When Clyde was going up for that interview — " She stopped. She said, "But that hasn't anything to do with it."

"I don't know," Bill said. "We never know, at this stage, what's important. Tell me what you were going to, Mrs. Wilmot."

"Nothing," she said. But then she appeared to reconsider. "I suppose I'd better," she said. "You'd think it was something important if I didn't, wouldn't you? It was when Clyde was trying to get into the diplomatic service. Like Mr. Monteath — the career service?"

"Yes," Bill said.

"It was several years ago," she said. "Clyde wanted it so much. He was so keyed up. He hadn't had a drink for — oh, months. We were all so pleased and — and hopeful. And then there was this interview."

She was not specific; she probably was not, Bill thought, a specific woman. There had been "this interview" with someone who would decide whether young Parsons could get into the service or stay out of it. Parsons had been nervous, wound up. And it had been Byron Wilmot who had suggested, who perhaps had even urged, that it was at such times that one particularly needed a drink. It had been Wilmot who had worked on Parsons's pride — told him to ignore all the old women who treated him like a baby; assured him that he could take a drink when he needed it, perhaps even a couple if he needed them, like anyone else. Like any other grown man. So, to steady himself, for the crucial interview, Parsons had taken a drink.

"He knew he shouldn't," Mrs. Wilmot said.

"But Byron — Byron *taunted* him. And so
— "

And so, it appeared, was not specifically said, young Parsons had turned up for the interview a little drunk, perhaps a good deal drunk. And that, not unreasonably, had been that. "A dreadful thing for Byron to do," Mrs. Wilmot said.

Bill nodded. He thought, but did not say, that perhaps Wilmot had, without too much intending it, served the larger good. A diplomat ought, surely, to be able to take a drink — to take even a couple of drinks.

"Go on about the party," Bill said, when Mrs. Wilmot stopped.

She went on, her account still fitting, not much amplifying, that of Pam and Jerry North. She told of the dummy's "murder."

"It wasn't as if Byron didn't know what it would mean to Mr. Monteath," she said. "To have it happen again."

She had said it before. It was time now to take it up. What had happened before of which the shooting of a red-wigged mannequin was a repetition?

Mrs. Wilmot seemed surprised at the question. She said, "Why, the burglar, of course" and waited as if, with that, she had explained everything. But Bill Weigand only shook his head. "But the police knew all about it," she said. "I thought of course — "

"No," Bill said. "You mean Mr. Monteath shot at a burglar once before? Under circumstances similar to this — this contrivance of Mr. Wilmot's?"

She did. She had assumed that the police, as represented by Captain Weigand, knew about that. It was, it had to be, a matter of record. Bill could only shake his head again. Perhaps some policemen knew; he did not. Where had it happened?

"Oh," she said. "Up in Maine. About — well, it was just before the war."

She was invited to go on. She went on.

The Wilmots had been motoring in Maine in late July of, she thought, 1940 or 1941. They had come to a little village near the coast — she paused at that, and shook her head. "I've forgotten the name of the place," she said. Byron Wilmot had remembered suddenly — told her he remembered suddenly — that the Monteaths had a cottage somewhere near, and had suggested they look the Monteaths up. "I remember I wasn't very enthusiastic," she said. "I didn't know them well at all and we'd planned to spend the night somewhere quite a ways ahead and — Well, anyway, Byron insisted."

They found the Monteaths' cottage after a little search, found it isolated, on a just passable road which ended with the cottage, and near the sea. They had found Monteath there alone.

"Right away I knew we shouldn't have come," she said. "He was so obviously worried and he was packing up. You see, his wife had been taken ill suddenly and was in a hospital in Portland. He had taken her there, I think, and then come back to pack up because — well, she was very ill."

Mrs. Wilmot had felt they were in the way, even though Monteath politely urged them to stay, to have a drink. They had, but over her protests. They had left in the late afternoon and driven on. "I still remember how worried poor Arthur was about his wife," she said. "How I felt we had intruded." She paused. "It was that same night it happened," she said. "We read about it in a newspaper the next day, or heard it on the car radio. I don't remember. Somebody tried to break into the cottage and Mr. Monteath shot to frighten him off. But — well, he killed him. Just by accident, of course. Not meaning to at all. You can imagine how he must have felt — his wife dying and then — this awful — mistake. And for Byron to bring it all up again last night!" She shook her head; she made a small sound, deprecating without words.

"Mrs. Monteath died?" Weigand asked.

She nodded. Mrs. Monteath — her name had been Grace — had died a day or two later in the hospital.

"Of course," she said, "everybody knew it — the shooting, I mean — had been an accident and the police didn't do anything to Arthur. Didn't arrest him or anything. Of course, they wouldn't. I don't suppose he could ever forget, though. The two things coming at the same time, that way and — and everything."

"The man he shot," Bill said. "Was he identified, do you know?"

She didn't.

"Did your husband?"

So far as she knew, Byron Wilmot had known no more than she.

"It hasn't anything to do with this, has it?" she asked. "I mean — I told you about it to show what — well, the kind of cruel things Byron would do. Do deliberately."

Bill Weigand understood that. There was no reason to think that this unfortunate accident of almost fifteen years ago had anything to do with Byron Wilmot's death.

"To get back to the party," he said. "After the incident of the dummy, do you remember anything that might help us?"

She told what else she remembered, which

133

brought little new. Her story of the last few minutes of the party accorded with that of the Norths', her account of her unsuccessful effort to get Clyde Parsons to go home with her agreed with his. She had taken a cab — she did not remember of what fleet, if any — from downtown New York to Forest Hills, getting home late. She had gone to bed. She waited, then. She was thanked. She went to the door with Bill Weigand and Mullins, stood on the porch watching them as they got into the car. Somewhere, in a shadowy marsh, peepers started their shrill salute to spring.

VI

Thursday, 3:55 P.M. *to* 5:15 P.M.

Mrs. Gerald North had telephoned, requesting that she be called back. A patient, bar-to-bar check had placed Clyde Parsons until around a quarter of two that morning — at which time he had been too intoxicated to be served at a small place on Eighth Street. (Or so the night bartender, pursued to his home in the Bronx and awakened there, had virtuously insisted.) Bill started another check, which would require equal patience: Did some hack driver's record show a trip, beginning at around one in the morning, from downtown New York to Forest Hills? Bill Weigand regarded Mullins. After consideration, he nodded. He gestured toward a telephone.

"See what Maine can tell us, sergeant," he said. Mullins groaned faintly, pointed out that Maine was large, the shooting of a stray burglar far in the past. But he got on with it.

Bill asked for a familiar number, heard the sound symbolic of a telephone's ringing, heard Pam North's voice. He listened.

"No," he said, "we haven't anybody following Baker." He listened again. He said,

"You're sure?" He listened. He said, "All right, Pam, I know you do. You do look at things." Once more he listened to a clear, quick voice. "I haven't the faintest idea," he said. "I'll try to get one. You said the Waldorf?"

That, Pam told him, was what Mr. Arthur Monteath had said to the cab driver, as he left to be followed by Mr. John Baker.

"I — " Pam said. "Wait a minute. Somebody's at the door. Shall I call you back?"

"Yes," Bill said. "No — wait a minute, Pam. I'll call you. Right?"

"Right," Pam North said, and the receiver clicked to Bill Weigand's ear. He looked toward Mullins, at another desk. Mullins was regarding a telephone with the expression of one who awaits a summons.

"Pam says our friend Baker is following Monteath," Bill said. "And that Monteath took the Norths to lunch to pump them. That Clyde Parsons wanted to get into the diplomatic service and didn't. That Monteath would like us to ask him whatever questions we have so he can go to Washington. That she forgot to ask him whether he knew anybody with red hair."

"Jeeze," Mullins said. His telephone rang. He said, "Mullins speaking." He said, "O.K., keep trying." He hung up.

"Put Stein on that," Bill told him. Mullins brightened. "Get up to the Waldorf. Find out if Monteath's stopping there. Find out if he is there. If Baker's there."

"O.K., Loot," Mullins said. He was pleased; detectives should not be chained to telephones. He went in search of Stein. Bill sat for a moment, his fingers tapping his desk, his eyes narrowed. If Pam North was right — and Pam was very often right — people were up to things. That was, he hoped, a good sign. He nodded to Stein, who came to attend Mullins's telephone, who would already be briefed. Bill Weigand got his car, drove to the Novelty Emporium. There he sought, and found, Mr. Dewsnap — Mr. Bertram Dewsnap.

Mr. Dewsnap was a small, gray man, and there was no merriment in him — among false faces of most hilarious design, tricks designed to convulse the most dour, Mr. Dewsnap gave no indication that he was amused, or ever had been. He sighed deeply when Bill identified himself.

"I can't understand it," he said, and tears trickled in his voice, although his sharp gray eyes remained entirely dry. "Mr. Wilmot was always so — so full of life." He sighed again. "Why, only yesterday — " He paused, he shook his head, he sighed once more. Bill

137

waited. "But there is no use remembering," Mr. Dewsnap told him. "We must learn to face it."

"Yes," Bill said. "I'd like to ask you a few questions, Mr. Dewlap."

"*Snap*," Dewsnap said. "Dew*snap*, captain."

Bill apologized; was told, in a tone of resignation, that it often happened. He was told, also, that there were already men going over the company's books. "Men from the police," Dewsnap said, and added a sound akin to "tut." Bill knew that; that was routine. He sought more personal background — specifically, the background data which might be available on Martha Evitts and John Baker.

Neither of whom was there, Dewsnap told him. He sighed again. He could not understand it. Baker had been there that morning; had gone to offer the police, in behalf of the staff, any assistance he could. ("I talked to him," Bill said.) Baker had not returned. Miss Evitts had simply not appeared. They had tried to get in touch with her at her apartment. They had failed. ("Right," Bill said. "So did we.")

"I can't understand it," Dewsnap said. "It's all quite — quite beyond me, captain."

"Yes," Bill said. "It's very difficult. Do you have personnel files, Mr. Dewsnap? I suppose you have?"

Mr. Dewsnap, without happiness, agreed that they had. He left the little office, which was on a mezzanine, with its only window overlooking a sales floor filled with the preposterous. He returned, after a few moments, with two folders. He proffered them to Weigand, suggested that his desk be used, left again. He reappeared on the floor below, moving among counters, among costume racks, his head turning from side to side as he walked.

Evitts — Martha Jean. Age 29. Employed at the Emporium for the past three years. An uptown address. Two former employers, with one of which she had remained three years, with the other two and a half. Letters of recommendation from both. High school graduate, two years' college, business school course completed. Parents — William and Martha Evitts — both deceased. Religion, protestant. Social security number — Bill made a note of it. Salary — the Emporium paid rather well. Next of kin — a cousin, one Mrs. Ralph Simpson, living in California. Bill made a note of her address.

He put the folder aside. It did not appear to have told him anything of importance. He took the other.

Baker — John. Age, 25. Address, a midtown hotel. Employed since the previous August. Salary — $50 weekly.

139

And — that was all. The folder held only a single file card, only so much information as might, without crowding, go on three lines of the card. Well, Bill Weigand thought. Well. Well. He went to the window which looked down on the sales floor. Mr. Dewsnap was looking up at it, which was convenient, if perhaps a little odd. Bill beckoned. Dewsnap came upstairs to the mezzanine, into his office. Bill abandoned the desk to its owner. He said, "Oughtn't there to be more than this about Mr. Baker?"

He showed Dewsnap the card. Dewsnap looked at it.

"Of course," he said. "Much more. I — " he paused. "I don't understand it," he said. "I don't understand it at all, captain. Unless — I'll look."

He went. He returned.

"I thought the rest might have slipped out," he said. "I can't find anything more. It's very — irregular."

"Yes," Bill said. "By the way — is that his present salary?"

Dewsnap looked at the card again. He said he would suppose so. He said that Mr. Wilmot had fixed salaries.

"It isn't much," Bill said.

Dewsnap looked at it again.

"No," he said. "It isn't very much, is it?

He must have to live very carefully."

Bill Weigand nodded. He considered. Were the personnel records kept in a locked file? They were not. Then anybody — any employee, certainly — could examine them? If he wished, add to them, subtract from them?

"Why?" Mr. Dewsnap asked. "I suppose so. But I don't understand, captain."

The area of Mr. Dewsnap's non-understanding seemed large. Did he really, Bill wondered, fail to understand what was surely obvious — that Baker, if he chose, could have taken from his record such information as he preferred the police, under these circumstances, not to come upon? Bill looked at Dewsnap with some care.

"You mean Mr. Baker might have taken out part of his records?" Mr. Dewsnap asked.

"Right," Bill said. "Mr. Baker. Or — someone else."

Mr. Dewsnap shook his head. He shook it worriedly, to all appearances a man out of his depth. "Why would anybody do that?" he asked.

Bill abandoned it. He said there was another thing.

"We found carbons of correspondence in Mr. Wilmot's apartment," he said. "Several in German, apparently arranging for the manufacture, in Germany, of certain devices. Do you know about that?"

Mr. Dewsnap's face cleared. That he did know about. A number of what the captain called "devices" — and the word was well chosen, certainly — were manufactured in Germany on designs developed by Mr. Wilmot or other inventors. Devices in which precision was of great importance, for the most part. Bill raised his eyebrows. Didn't the import duties —

"Mr. Wilmot apparently thought not," Mr. Dewsnap said. "He is — was — a very astute businessman, captain."

"He would send the designs to Germany?" Bill said. "Those were the blueprints, I suppose?"

"I haven't seen the ones you're talking about," Dewsnap said. "But — yes, that was the way it was done. The designs, and specifications. Chiefly for magic devices." He paused. "To western Germany, of course," he added.

Bill said, without emphasis, that he had supposed so. He went to talk briefly to the men who were going through files. One of them shrugged. "Did a good business," he said. "What are we looking for?" Bill could not tell them that, beyond what they knew of that. "Anything that doesn't fit," he said. "Incidentally — if you come across personnel records of a man named John Baker, I'd like to see them. Some stuff seems to be missing." He got an, "O.K., captain."

From the floor below, on his way elsewhere, he looked up at the window of the office on the mezzanine. Mr. Dewsnap was looking down intently. Bill raised a hand, but Dewsnap did not appear to notice it. He was looking, Bill realized, not at a departing detective but at a man who had just come through the door from the street. Bill looked at the man.

The man was of medium height, medium build. There did not seem to be anything in his appearance to occasion the intent scrutiny Dewsnap was giving him. Nevertheless, on the chance, Bill himself committed a face to memory — a long face, thinnish, an almost imperceptible scar-tracing running diagonally through the left eyebrow, irregular teeth. Hair, gray. Bill had passed the newcomer by then, but the picture remained with him. Hair, not altogether gray. Probably had been red.

For an instant, Bill checked his stride. Then he resumed it. It was true that, some years before, the man he had just passed probably had had red hair. So, however, had a very considerable minority of the population, even if red-haired mannequins were not included. Still —

He crossed the street to a drugstore, made

a telephone call. He sat at a soda counter, drank coffee, watching the entrance to the Novelty Emporium. After about ten minutes, a man came in and bought cigarettes. He lighted one. He became interested in a display of pocket-size reprints. He was a man with time on his hands — time to waste. Well, Bill thought, he was almost certainly wasting it. Bill smiled to himself. Pam North would be pleased, when he told her. She had thought red hair so important.

Bill retrieved his car and drove across town to a residential hotel in the Chelsea area. Mr. John Baker was not in. Several people had been trying to get in touch with him.

The hotel was small; it was well kept. Bill indicated that he might be looking for a place to stay, perhaps for several weeks. A room with bath, by the week or, possibly, by the month? A very pleasant room, in the rear, where it was quiet, would cost a hundred and twenty-five a month. A room similar to Mr. Baker's? Quite similar. Mr. Baker did, of course, have a corner room. Such a room, if one were available — none was, at the moment — would naturally cost a little more.

Bill would let him know. He would get in touch with Mr. Baker at his office.

It appeared that Mr. Baker had a private income or a very small appetite. He was spending considerably more than half his salary for lodging. It also appeared, at the moment, that Mr. Baker had no past. It was possible, of course, that he was carrying his past in his pocket.

Bill went back to his office. Sergeant Stein had been efficient, and lucky. The Maine state police had been efficient, and cooperative. Stein stopped typing his report and gave Weigand an oral summary.

At about one in the morning of July 28, 1940, Arthur Monteath had been alone in his cottage, near the sea, near Pemaquid. He had been awakened by the sound of someone trying to force the door — someone who, apparently, had thought the cottage empty. Confronted, the man had turned threatening. Monteath had fired one shot from a .32 automatic, intending to miss, to frighten. But, half asleep, nervously upset because of his wife's sudden illness — for whatever reason — Monteath had not missed. He had shot the intruder through the forehead. Discovering what he had done, he had at once telephoned the police, told them the story, produced a permit for the pistol.

There had been nothing, no uncertainty in the story, no physical evidence, to lead to doubt. There is no law which says a man may not defend his home, himself. All that

Monteath said, all he showed in manner, convinced the police that only a warning shot had been intended. Monteath had not been arrested, there had been no court action.

The dead man had been identified as Joseph Parks, twenty-four years old. He had lived in New York. He had a police record — juvenile delinquency, 1932; a charge of grand larceny, 1936, acquitted; extortion, 1938, sentenced to three years, on parole at time of death. There was nothing to make it improbable that he had taken to burglarizing summer cottages. He had never been a particularly successful outlaw.

Mrs. Monteath had, as Mrs. Wilmot had said, died in a Portland hospital the morning of the twenty-ninth. She had had a heart attack at the cottage, and a second at the hospital. She had been twenty-eight years old. The Monteaths had been married only two years.

"Things piled up on the poor guy," Stein said.

Weigand agreed that they had indeed. And it was, presumably, of those few tragic days in late July of 1940 that Byron Wilmot had elected to remind Monteath. Or — had he?

"Parks have red hair?" Bill asked. "Look like this mannequin of Wilmot's?"

Stein had not seen the mannequin. Neither had Bill Weigand, and the Norths' description had not been detailed — beyond the red hair. Stein went through his notes. He shook his head. Parks had been a heavy-set young man, black-haired, ruddy complexion.

"How did they identify Parks?"

"Prints. Oh yes — somebody who'd known him showed up. Man named" — he returned to the notes — "Behren." He spelled it. "Alexander Behren."

The name meant nothing. "Have red hair?" Weigand asked, a little to his own surprise.

"Now captain," Stein said. "Have a heart."

"Right," Bill said. "Forget it."

Although the afternoon was warm for so early in the spring, Martha Evitts had stood shivering in the doorway to the Norths' apartment. She had hugged a cloth coat about her. Her face had been pale; her brown eyes inordinately large. She had said, "I had to come. I had to — " and had broken off, and swayed a little in the doorway. Pam had gone to her quickly. Martha Evitts's body was shaking, as with the cold. But it was not cold. In the apartment it was very warm.

"I had to come to someone," she had said. "I've got to find out."

But Pam had told her to wait; had said she needed something hot; had got her tea, very hot, and had poured brandy into it. Martha

147

had sat on the edge of a deep chair; the cup had trembled in her hand as she raised it to her lips. She held the cup in both hands, then, as if to warm her hands. She put the cup down and made her slender hands into fists, to bring them warmth.

"I don't know what to do," she said. "I — "

"Drink your tea first," Pam said. "You want something else?"

Martha shook her head. She sipped again, finished the cup, nodded when Pam offered to refill it. The second cup, laced again with brandy, did more. Color came back to Martha Evitts's face; the hand which lifted the cup grew steadier.

"I've been walking around all day," she said then. "I — I don't know where. I didn't know where to go. Then I thought — she'll know. She was there too."

"You mean the penthouse," Pam said. "Yes. Oh — it was in the papers, wasn't it?"

Martha nodded.

"I went there," she said. Her voice still shook a little. She drank again from the cup. "I had a key. To take dictation, you know. And — and — "

"I know," Pam said. "I saw, too. You didn't tell anybody?"

Martha shook her head. The movement was

quick. "I couldn't," she said. "How could I?"

Pam merely waited.

"He was dead then," Martha said.

"Yes," Pam said. "He had been dead for — oh, for several hours."

"The papers said that. Didn't they — just *say* that? Didn't the police — *Mrs. North. Have they arrested John?*"

"No," Pam said. She paused. "Anyway, I don't think — I don't think they've arrested anybody."

"I think they have," she said. "I've — I've been trying to find him. I have to find him. Where is he? You know. Somebody must — " She stopped. "I don't know why I say that," she said. "I — "

She stopped. Her effort to gain control of herself was physical, evident in the muscles of slim hands, in the movements of facial muscles.

"I have to tell somebody," she said. "Not the police. Not yet. I wanted to see John first but I can't find him. He'd be able to explain what — " She stopped again. "Mr. Wilmot had really been dead for — for a long time? When I found him?"

"Six hours, anyway," Pam said. "Perhaps longer. Why is it so important?"

"I can't — " Martha said, and again she hesitated. She leaned forward a little in the chair. "But if that's true, I was wrong," she said. "Wasn't I?"

"I don't know what you mean," Pam said. "I'm sorry. How can I?"

"You were there after I was," Martha said. "It must have been — oh, only a short time. Isn't that true?"

"Yes," Pam said. "You came down and, because of the way you looked, I knew something must be wrong. The elevator man and I went up."

"You saw me come down?" Martha said. She shook her head. "I didn't see anybody."

"You could have touched me," Pam said. "I had a big package of groceries. You didn't see me?"

"No," Martha said. "It doesn't matter. You saw John too, then?"

"Mr. Baker? No. You were by yourself. You — "

"Not there." Martha was impatient. "I'm getting it all mixed up. In the penthouse."

Pam shook her head.

"I thought you had," Martha said. "I kept walking around, calling John's hotel and not getting him, calling the office and — I was sure you'd seen him. Told the police. That the police had arrested him and were — were making him talk. I — all day I'd see them — the light and

— and men hitting him and — "

"They don't do that," Pam said. She hesitated. "Not Bill's people," she said, firmly. "Mr. Baker was in Mr. Wilmot's apartment when you went in?"

"On the terrace," Martha said. "Outside. Looking into the room. He must have seen me and — and I thought he had just come and found Mr. Wilmot before I did. But — but then he disappeared. I don't know where. But if he'd just found the body and saw me he'd — he'd have come to me. Then, when he didn't — when he just wasn't there — I thought — Mr. Wilmot did a bad thing to us last night. A dreadful thing. John was — " She stopped.

"Mr. Wilmot had been dead for hours when you saw Mr. Baker," Pam said.

"I thought that wasn't true. But then, why did he just — leave me? Not come when — it was a shock, of course. I needed him, Mrs. North. If he had found Mr. Wilmot, and that was all, why did — why can't I find him anywhere? Why didn't *he* call the police?"

She looked at Pam North and her big eyes were dark, demanding of reassurance.

"Because — " Pam began, and then stopped. The girl, back now on the edge of the deep chair, waited, waited with a kind of desperation. But in the end, Pam North

151

could only shake her head.

It was not that there was no answer. There was an immediate answer: John Baker had not just reached the penthouse when Martha saw him there; he had not innocently found the body of his employer. He had seen Martha Evitts, had assumed that she would at once call the police; had not waited for the police. The explanation was not difficult; it was merely one she could not offer the dark-eyed young woman who sat so tensely across from her; to whom it would come, in any case, as but a confirmation of what she already desperately feared.

The girl swayed in her chair. Pam moved to go to her, but Martha Evitts took the chair arms in her hands, and steadied herself, and said she would be all right.

"I didn't sleep much last night," she said. "John took me to the apartment but I couldn't sleep and — it's a small apartment and two other girls share it with me. So I dressed again and went to an all-night diner and had some coffee and — and tried to get John on the telephone at his hotel. But he didn't answer and — " She broke off. "I'm older than John," she said. "You saw that. Too old for him. That was why — "

"I know," Pam said. "You're not — it's not just chronological."

"John says that," Martha said. "Says it over and over. He wasn't home last night, Mrs. North. This morning, I mean. I telephoned again, and it must have been four this morning and they rang his room but he didn't answer and — "

She leaned back, suddenly. And closed her eyes. Her hands gripped tight on the arms of the chair.

"I'm afraid," she said. "I'm terribly afraid. They've arrested John."

"No," Pam said.

The girl merely shook her head.

"No," Pam said. "Listen to me. *No*. This afternoon, Mr. Baker wasn't arrested. A few hours ago. He was in a car, driving the car. He drove out of the parking garage opposite the Algonquin and he was alone. Nobody else was in the car. He — " Pam North checked herself.

The doorbell rang. Cats, who had withdrawn to another room on Martha Evitts's arrival, came galloping to attend. Pam North crossed the living room, opened the door, and looked up at John Baker — at the open, youthful face of John Baker, at the smiling face.

"Well," Pam North said. "Of all people. *No, Teeney, you can't!*" She stopped the cat named Teeney with a quick, experienced foot.

Teeney looked at Pam sharply, spoke

153

sharply, communicated — by means not clear to humans — with her daughters. The three cats, in a line, Sherry moving like a hobby-horse, galloped from the living room.

"I'm sorry to bother you," John Baker said. "They told me Captain Weigand might — "

The chair in which Martha Evitts sat had presented a high back to the door. Martha came out of the chair; she crossed the room, running, almost stumbling. She said, *"John! Oh, John!"* She was in John Baker's arms. "I've been looking everywhere," she said, her voice muffled, her face against his coat. "I was so frightened." Baker held her close. But he looked over her head at Pamela North and his eyes narrowed.

His face changed then, or to Pam seemed to. It was no longer so youthful, so open. For an instant it was an older face, more experienced — and harder. But this expression — if she had not imagined it — passed quickly.

"You didn't need to be," Baker told Martha. "What would happen to me?" He held her off, looked down at her, smiled. "What?" he repeated. She shook her head and smiled at him. Her smile was uncertain.

"She thought the police might have happened to you, Mr. Baker," Pam North said. "She thought rubber hoses and glaring lights."

Baker's expression could not have been

154

more open, more ingenuous.

"The police?" he repeated. "Why on earth?" He looked down at the girl. "Why on earth, Martha?" he said.

"Because she saw you in the penthouse this morning," Pam North said. "When she found Mr. Wilmot. You were there, on the terrace."

John Baker stepped a little away from Martha, then. He kept an arm around her shoulders, held her lightly, emphasizing — but it seemed to Pam unconsciously emphasizing — their unity. And he said, "Oh," in a flat voice, an entirely non-committal voice. He removed his arm, then, and turned so he faced Martha. He smiled at her again, but it was a thinner smile. (His whole face, Pam thought, had become thinner. And this time the change was not fleeting.) "Yes," he said. "Well, I was afraid you had. I was rather afraid you had."

He's not at all what I thought he was, Pam thought. Not the least bit what I thought he was. And then she thought, *what he wants people to think he is.*

"You've told Mrs. North," he said, still to Martha Evitts. "Anyone else, Martha?"

There was no special feeling revealed in his voice.

Martha shook her head, her soft brown hair swinging just a little with the movement. Her eyes were wide again, the smile was no longer on her gentle mouth. She said, "Nobody, John."

"You *were* there, then?" Pam said, and he turned to her with, apparently, a moment of surprise.

"Of course," he said. He smiled faintly, thinly. "Martha is a very truthful person, Mrs. North," he said.

"I had to tell someone," Martha said. "I had to. I was so — so alone. So afraid."

"Yes," he said. "I'm sorry. You needn't have been." He put a hand on her shoulder. "It's all right, Martha," he said. "Nothing to be afraid of."

But then he turned back to Pam North. He looked at her, considered her.

"You've told Weigand?" he said. She shook her head. "That means, 'not yet,' " he told her. He did not ask a question, but accepted the self-evident. There was nothing frightening in his voice, Pam told herself. There was nothing in his voice at all. I should really not be frightened, Pam North thought, and thereupon was.

"It will be inconvenient," he said. He smiled again, notably without warmth. "You're rather an inconvenient person, Mrs. North."

"She's kind," Martha Evitts said. "I tell you, she's kind. Couldn't you tell last night

156

when — when she understood what Mr. Wilmot had done? She won't — "

"Oh yes, Martha," Baker said. "She will, of course. As soon as she can get Captain Weigand on the telephone."

"He's coming here," Pam said, quickly. "You said yourself — started to say when you first came in — that someone had told you he might be here already."

"I did, didn't I?" Baker said. "Well, I had to say something, Mrs. North."

"You didn't come for that, then?"

"Well," he said, "not entirely. No. I've no reason to think Weigand's coming here, at the moment."

"And not because Martha was here, because how could you have known?"

He nodded.

"Of course," he said, "I could have been watching the building, seen her come in, come up after her to see that she didn't — tell too much."

"No," Pam said. "Because, look at the time you'd have waited and what would have been the point? I mean, there was time enough for her to tell, wasn't there?"

Martha looked from one of them to the other, her large eyes questioning.

"No," he said. "Nobody's watching the house, so far as I know. No reason anyone

157

should now, is there?"

"Then?"

"Suppose we say," he suggested, "that I'm very concerned about Mr. Wilmot's death — admired him a lot, you know. I'm very anxious, suppose we say, to know what's being done to find the man who killed him. I don't want to bother the police, who are busy men, but I remember that you and Mr. North are friends of Captain Weigand, and have — suppose we say? — been associated with him in a few cases and — "

"Suppose," Pam North said, "we don't say anything of the kind, Mr. Baker?"

"No?" Baker said. "Why not?"

"Because it isn't that simple," Pam said. "Because earlier this afternoon you were following Mr. Monteath and — " She stopped, because, unexpectedly, he smiled again. It was not a cordial smile. It was, however, revealing.

"*That's* what you came to find out," Pam said. "Whether we'd seen you following Mr. Monteath. Isn't it?"

"Well," Baker said, "perhaps that, among other things. Yes. You told Weigand?"

"Yes."

He looked at her, his eyes again narrowing.

"You *are* a rather inconvenient person,

158

Mrs. North," he said. "You manage — or will manage — to focus a good deal of attention on me, I'm afraid."

"You don't want that, do you?"

"It's inconvenient," he said. "Not, suppose we say, according to plan. But none of it is, I'm afraid. It's all — "

"*John!*" Martha Evitts said. "You don't — you don't know anything about Mr. Wilmot? *Tell me!*"

"Why yes," he said, "I know quite a bit about Mr. Wilmot. But — that isn't what you mean, is it?"

She shook her head, the soft hair swaying.

"No," Baker said. "I didn't kill him, Martha. I'd have been the last man to do that, just now." He smiled at her, and this time smiled more gently. "Not that he's a great loss," he said. "To anybody."

"You didn't go back to your hotel this morning," Martha said. "I called and called. I was — you were so angry — so — so different. Because of what he did to us."

"I was," Baker said. "That was personal, Martha. We can't help having personal — " He stopped. "No," he said, "I wasn't at the hotel. I went there but — it was necessary to leave again. But I didn't go to Wilmot's place. Not then. I rather wish I had."

They both looked at him.

"Not to kill him," he said. "He's no use dead."

"Use?" Pam North said. "No use?"

"None at all," Baker said. "Of course, that may have been the idea. Probably was."

Pam didn't, she said, understand what he was talking about. She was told there was no reason she should; that none of it concerned her. "Directly," John Baker added. It would be a good idea for her to remember that.

"It would be a very good idea," he said, and again his voice had a peculiar lack of any emphasis whatever. "You don't want to get hurt."

It was not a threat; it was no more than a statement — a statement of the obvious. But detachment can, in its fashion, be threatening.

"I — " Pam began, but John Baker did not listen. He put a hand on Martha Evitts's arm, and the touch did not seem to be a caress. He turned her toward the door. She said, "Wait, John, we can't — " but by then he had opened the door, was shaking his head.

"Come on," he said. "There's nothing to do here."

Martha did not obviously hold back against the compelling hand. But Pam North felt, nonetheless, that she went reluctantly with Baker, went with doubt and in uncertainty.

160

In the hall outside Baker turned to speak over his shoulder. He told Pam to take care of herself. It might have been a cliché of parting. Perhaps, Pam thought, that's all it is.

VII

Thursday, 4:55 P.M. *to* 6:10 P.M.

The telephone rang. Mullins reported from the Waldorf — Arthur Monteath was registered there, but did not answer his room telephone. John Baker was not to be seen in the public rooms. Should he have Monteath paged?

"No," Bill said. "Leave a message. Ask him to give us a ring. All very polite, sergeant. Then come in."

"O.K., Loot," Mullins said. "I mean — "

"Right," Bill said. "Come in."

Bill returned to reports. The technical men, and the others, had finished at the Wilmot apartment, the door of which had then been sealed. Dust from the floors, from the furniture, was under microscopes. Fingerprints of a dozen people — of twenty — were being checked. The former occupant of the apartment was in the morgue, perhaps under knives of pathologists. Papers from the apartment — Bill's eyebrows went up. A man who had an office in Foley Square had appeared, had talked briefly with an assistant commissioner of police, had departed, taking with him the

162

blueprints which had been among the papers, and certain of the carbons of Mr. Wilmot's correspondence.

The last will and testament of Byron Wilmot, if any, was not among the papers in his apartment. It was not in his private file at the Emporium. His lawyer's name had been. His lawyer had drawn up no will for Byron Wilmot. So far as the lawyer knew, Clyde Parsons was Wilmot's closest — indeed, his only — blood relative. If no will turned up, no closer relative — yes, Parsons would inherit. Bill changed the order of the reports, took up the one concerned with the movements of Clyde Parsons the night before.

A gap remained. Mr. Parsons disappeared from view at a little before two in the morning, when he went thirsty — if one could believe the bartender — from a grill in Eighth Street. He reappeared, something over two hours later, at the outside door of the building, west of Eighth Avenue, in which he rented a two-room flat. He appeared there, swaying, and found the outside door locked. He discovered, apparently, that he had lost his key.

"Locked after midnight," the superintendent explained. "Got to in this neighborhood." He had waved his hand to indicate a neighborhood which, to the enquiring detective, had looked quiet enough. The detective knew neighborhoods —

"Tenants got their own keys," the super-intendent said. "See?"

The detective saw.

"Except this guy Parsons, he's got to lose his key," the superintendent said. "Got to lose it four o'clock in the morning. Got to stand there, leaning on the button, till he wakes me up. And the wife. So there he is, stinking drunk, saying something you can't make out about the key. And his coat. No coat either."

"Topcoat, you mean?"

"What else'd I mean? No topcoat. So he thinks, as I make it out, the key was in the topcoat and — phooey. No hat, either."

"You let him in?"

"Sure I let him in. He falls going upstairs. Man, was he drunk!"

"And that was?"

"Four-ten. Fifteen, maybe. Somewhere around there."

The lost key unlocked not only the outer door of the building's entrance hall, but the door to Parsons's flat. The superintendent had climbed with Parsons — three flights — and let him in there. It had been, not in short, "a hell of a thing."

"Seems to have been," the detective had said, and gone to simmer it into a report.

So — two hours unaccounted for; a significant two hours; two hours which Parsons himself had been unable to account for. So — a missing topcoat Parsons had not mentioned. So — Parsons inherited, probably. There was twenty-eight thousand, seven hundred and fifty to inherit, to begin with.

Bill reverted to the report on that. The money had been in old bills. It could not in any fashion be traced. Inside the safe there had been Wilmot's fingerprints, recently made. There had been, further, a set of fingerprints, probably even more recently made, which were not Wilmot's. Nor were they the prints of the expert who had opened the safe. They were not the prints of anyone known to the New York City police. A code description of them had gone to Washington.

Bill Weigand looked at nothing, and let his fingers tap the desk. Somebody — but when? — had had his hands in Wilmot's safe. (The right hand, at any rate; three fingers of the right hand.) The somebody — but why? — had not been interested in twenty-eight thousand, seven hundred and fifty dollars. Or, had there been more money there? Had part of the hoard been taken?

The questions were obvious. It would be pleasant, Bill thought, to find a few of the answers. He went on with it.

Sylvester Frank, Wilmot's servant — the

butler who had trained himself to annoy, because he knew it teased — was as annoying now as he had ever been. He teased by the most simple method — that of complete disappearance. At a little after ten that morning he had gone to the penthouse. He had, obviously, found his employer dead. If he had done anything about this, it did not appear. He had gone from there. It was possible, but unlikely, that he had merely gone to look for another job. A pickup was out on him, he was wanted for questioning. Bill Weigand thought about him. He wondered whether, until then, he had thought enough about him. He read again what others had found out about Sylvester Frank.

Frank was thirty-four years old. He had been born in Hoboken. He had started as a waiter, in Hoboken, when he was nineteen. He had become a comic waiter some five years later. And, as a comic waiter, he had enjoyed a certain renown. He had made a very good thing out of insulting those he served; he had been inventive at it, and in demand at public dinners of a certain kind. Yet, five years before, he had abandoned a career which combined profit with innocent merriment, and had gone to work for Wilmot. It was to be assumed that he had been comic only at Wilmot's parties; it was unlikely that, dining alone, Wilmot

166

had encouraged his servant to serve soup with a thumb in it. In short, Frank had abandoned a career and gone to work.

It would, Bill decided, be interesting to know why. It would be interesting to know whether Frank had, in the end, found his employer too trying to be put up with. It would be interesting to know what Frank had been about between two-thirty and, say, six that morning. But you cannot question a man you haven't caught. Bill put Sylvester Frank aside. He turned to Martha Evitts.

Miss Evitts had reached her uptown apartment a little before two, arousing one of her apartment mates, a girl who was "waked up by the least little thing." The light sleeper, one Paula Thompson, had gone back to light sleeping, only to be again awakened, after about half an hour, by the sounds of Martha Evitts's departure from the apartment. "Where you going at this time of night?" Paula asked, but was not heard, or at any rate not answered. Martha had come back at about three-thirty, awakening Paula once more. Then, after breakfast — of which she ate little — Miss Evitts had disappeared, so it had been impossible for Paula to ask what had made her so restless in the night, or where she had gone in the night.

The telephone rang. Was this Captain William Weigand? Then, one moment please, Mr. Monteath was calling. After the moment, Bill confirmed his identity to Mr. Monteath, confirmed also that he had asked Monteath to telephone. He explained that, in connection with the unfortunate death of his friend Wilmot —

"Not my friend particularly," Monteath said. "But go on, captain."

The police liked, Bill went on, to find out all they could, even from people who knew little. He wondered whether he might stop by and see Mr. Monteath, and ask the few routine questions, necessary.

"Now?" Monteath said.

"Right," Bill told him. "As good a time as any for me, Mr. Monteath."

Monteath hesitated. He was at someone's office. He could not tell exactly when he would be leaving. If Captain Weigand was going to be at his own office for a time?

Indefinitely, Bill thought. For an hour or so, he told Monteath. Then, Monteath would come around as soon as he could manage. "Get it over with," he said. "I want to get down to Washington tomorrow."

"Right," Bill said, and told him where to come.

Bill returned to the reports. The night clerk at John Baker's hotel had been pursued to his small room near the top of the building, near the elevator shaft, and, awakened from hot sleep, had remembered Baker's return that morning. Baker had got in at about twenty minutes after two, and had picked up his key.

But — Baker had not remained in. Fifteen minutes later he had gone out again, taking his key with him. He had not returned by the time the night clerk went off — of that the night clerk professed himself certain. "Probably accurate," the precinct detective noted. "Have to pass the desk to get to elevator or stairs." Bill pictured the hotel lobby in his mind. If the night clerk had been at his station, and awake, he would almost certainly have seen Baker, had Baker returned. It was not, however, a point provable beyond reasonable doubt. (They were a long way from a place where reasonable doubt mattered. Bill was not certain that they were, at the moment, getting appreciably closer.)

Bill remembered John Baker as he had come a little after noon — had come fresh-faced, open-faced, to offer his assistance, and that of the staff of the Novelty Emporium. Baker had not looked like a man who had spent the night out. He had been freshly shaved, had appeared rested. He could have been to a barber, obviously; he could be physically resilient. He could also have other lodging, or what amounted to other lodging. Baker, Bill Weigand decided, was becoming a man of discrepancies. It would be necessary, before long, to reconcile him.

Simultaneously, the telephone on Bill's desk rang and Sergeant Mullins came into the office. Bill acknowledged the arrival of Mullins, identified himself to the telephone. A voice said, "Saul Bessing, Bill."

Bill Weigand said, "Hello, Saul. How are all the wonder boys?"

"Fine," Saul said. "Just fine. How's good old Arty?"

"Inspector O'Malley," Bill said with great formality, "is on a brief and well-earned leave."

"Must make things nice and quiet," Bessing said. "Hear you've got a tough one, Bill."

"Um-m-m," Bill said. "Do you?"

"Yes," Saul said. "About that first print your people sent through to Washington. Negative, Bill."

"Well, thanks," Bill said. "You're quick about it."

"Cooperation," Saul said. "We always cooperate. Cooperation between the various agencies of law enforcement is the sine qua non of — "

"Come off it," Bill said. "Washington goes to the trouble of hurrying things up. You go to the trouble of telephoning. In a rush to say you haven't got a print that went to Washington through routine channels — wait a minute. You do mean that?"

"What else?" Saul said. "In re, subject print. No information available."

"You know, Saul. I rather like 'available.' A nice evasive word."

"And here," Saul said, "we go to all the trouble of cooperating. And the thanks we get."

"Look, Saul," Bill said. "Tell me this much. You people are in on the Wilmot kill?"

"I hope not, Bill," Saul said. "We all hope not. We hope it was a nice personal job — so somebody could inherit his money, say. Nothing we'd care about. Nothing that would have — well, let's say have ramifications."

"Like blueprints of — devices — being sent to Germany?"

"Well," Saul said, "things like that might come into it, mightn't they?"

"For God's sake, Saul," Bill said. "Do you — "

The telephone on Sergeant Mullins's desk rang, distractingly. Mullins picked it up. He said, "The captain's on the other phone — oh, hello Mrs. North. Do you want — "

"Take it, Mullins," Bill said. Then, to Saul Bessing, "Do you have to be this way?"

"Well, I'll tell you," Saul said. "Let's put it like this. It would be convenient if your Mr. Wilmot got killed because somebody didn't like his taste in neckties. Or the kind of jokes he played. Something nice and clean and simple. Might happen to anybody who had bad taste in neckties. Nothing to disturb his business associates. They'd just say, 'Too bad about poor old Byron. If we told him about those neckties once, we told him a hundred times.' And then, maybe, they'd just get on with their business. See what I mean?"

"Probably," Bill said. "You're interested in this — 'business,' I gather? Don't want it interfered with?"

"Well," Saul said, "we'd hate to have any rumors — any unsubstantiated rumors, you know — get around that would upset anybody."

"We don't spread rumors," Bill told him. "You know that damn well."

"Sure," Saul said. "Only — the more people the more rumors, don't you think? Anyway, that's what the big boys think. I'm just a voice, pal."

"Security," Bill said, and made it sound an epithet. He was told not to use profanity. "Cooperation," Bill said.

"My dear captain," Saul Bessing said, "what

do you think we're giving you? Why do you think I called?"

"Right," Bill said. "You've probably done what you could. I'll grant that." He paused, momentarily. "It's rather odd about the print, isn't it?" he said. "You've got such a lot of them available."

"Oh," Bessing said, "we've missed one or two."

"Yes," Bill said. "By the way, did you ever hear of a man named Monteath — Arthur Monteath?"

"Seems as if I might have. State Department, isn't he? Seems as if I've heard the name."

"That's all?"

"That's all, Bill."

"A man named Sylvester Frank? A man named John Baker? A young woman named Martha Evitts? A man named Dewsnap?"

"You do meet a lot of interesting people in your work, don't you?" Saul Bessing said. "Well, been nice talking to you, pal."

And then Saul Bessing hung up. Bill Weigand glared at the telephone. Then he shrugged. Probably Saul had done what he could. He usually did. Bill turned to Mullins.

"Mrs. North," Mullins said. "Miss Evitts was there because she couldn't get in touch with Mr. Baker, and he was at the penthouse

173

this morning, but just now he was at Mrs. North's and he isn't at all what he appears to be and she's afraid — that's Mrs. North's afraid — what it really amounts to is he's snatched Miss Evitts." Mullins paused and blinked. "Maybe I could of got it mixed up a little," he said. "Sometimes she goes pretty fast."

"Yes," Bill said. "Sometimes she — "

The telephone rang again. The precinct man who had relieved Bill in a drugstore across from the Novelty Emporium reported, sadly. The gray-haired man, whose hair might once have been red, had emerged from the Emporium after about half an hour. He had been followed to a subway, in the subway to Times Square, in Times Square he had been lost. "In one door and out another," the detective said. "I'm sorry, captain. But you know how it is."

Bill did; one man can always be shaken. He can be shaken even without intention.

"You think he spotted you?" Bill asked.

"Not unless he was expecting someone. If he did — sure."

"Did he plan to shake you?"

"It's hard to tell, captain. But — yes, I'd guess he did. You want me to backtrack on him? At the store?"

"No," Bill said. "We'll skip it for now."

The detective was sorry about it. He was told he had done what he could.

"Mrs. North said to come around if you could," Mullins said.

"Right," Bill said.

He drummed on his desk with his fingers. There were a great many pieces; too many, it occurred to him, for a single jig-saw. It might be that he had pieces from two puzzles, scrambled together. That would be fine, Bill thought. That would be wonderful. And once more the telephone rang.

A Mr. Monteath was at the sergeant's desk downstairs. Did the captain want him sent up.

"I suppose so," Bill said, weariness in his voice. He pulled himself out of it. "Right," he said. "Send him up, sergeant." He waited, briefly. The office door opened, a voice said, "Right in here," and then, "Mr. Monteath to see you, captain."

Bill looked at Monteath. Then, unconsciously, he straightened his own tie, which had probably — from the feel had certainly — worked to one side. He became conscious of this and smiled faintly, wondered briefly whether Mr. Arthur Monteath so affected all the men he met, convicting them, in their own minds of lamentable sloppiness.

It was not that Monteath, standing easily in the doorway, coming easily to a chair when bidden, appeared to have gone to any particular trouble about dressing himself. Anyone — anyone, at least, who could find Mr. Monteath's tailor and pay the tailor's charge — might wear such a gray suit, with the faintest of chalk stripes. Anyone might find — or have made — a shirt with a collar so smoothly fitting and cuffs so just enough showing below jacket sleeves. No doubt gray and maroon ties of similar subtlety were widely available. There was nothing to indicate that Mr. Monteath had thought long about these matters, or gone to any particular trouble. One was left, rather, with the feeling that Mr. Monteath's clothes had merely happened to him because this had turned out to be his lucky day. Bill Weigand nevertheless straightened his necktie.

"Mrs. North said you probably would want to see me," Monteath said. "I'd been planning to get in touch with you." Bill nodded. "But I'm afraid there won't be much I can tell you."

"Anything you can," Bill told him. "We go around picking up pieces. Looking for them, anyway. Anything about Wilmot."

Monteath knew nothing about Wilmot, he was certain, that the police didn't already know. He had seen Wilmot only once in years, that once being the night before. "Unfortu-

nately," he added. "Bad for my — business."
He smiled faintly. "The Caesar's wife sort of
thing, if you know what I mean."

"Right," Bill said. "We appreciate that.
We'll try to make it as painless as we can.
You knew Wilmot rather well at one time?"

Not even that, Monteath said. He had gone
to college with Wilmot; seen him off and on
for a few years, not seen him for a dozen.
"I've been abroad most of the time," Monteath said. Then he looked puzzled. "Come
to think of it," he said, "I don't really know
how Wilmot found out I was back, and where
I was stopping. To invite me to this shindig of
his, I mean. I got a note — renew old acquaintance, that sort of thing. Few people in he
thought I might enjoy meeting. Hadn't anything else on, you know, so — well, there
you are. Rather, there I was."

"Right," Bill said. "Heard you were in town
from some mutual friend, you suppose?"

"I don't know who," Monteath said. "As
a matter of fact, I didn't know we had any.
But it must have been something like that."

"Probably," Bill said. "And it was quite a
— shindig, I gather."

"Phew!" Monteath said. "I've been to some
parties, pretty much all over. But — phew!"

He was invited to tell about the party. He
did, summarizing, organizing adeptly what

he had to tell, now — at home, obviously, in the *précis* — letting the details he furnished speak for themselves. The party came clearer to Weigand in outline, although the colors, so vivid in Pam North's narrative, faded somewhat. But little new was added.

" — thought this man was shooting at us," Monteath said. "Wilmot had told me he'd loaded up with blanks, so I fired to scare the man. Well — you can guess how I felt when he toppled over. Very — lifelike the whole thing was." He paused. "Deathlike would be a better word."

"An odd sort of joke for anyone to play," Bill said.

"Very. Shocking sort of — joke. Shocking taste, of course."

"This mannequin," Bill said. "I gather that Wilmot had gone to some trouble to make it — well, distinctive. As if he'd copied the face, from life. Did you feel that?"

"I didn't particularly then. Too much going on and I was — well, call it upset. Thrown off base, you know. But, as I think about it, I suppose one could say that."

"But it didn't remind you of anybody *you'd* known? Met before anywhere?"

Monteath appeared to be surprised. He shook his head. Then he stopped shaking it and looked at Bill Weigand with intentness.

178

"You've got something in mind, haven't you?" he asked.

"Not necessarily," Bill said. "It's an obvious question, Mr. Monteath."

Monteath continued to look at him. Then he appeared to make up his mind.

"Rather beating about the bush, aren't you?" he asked. "Why not come out with it?"

"Right," Bill said. "This trick rather — well, it was a little a case of history repeating itself, wasn't it? I'm talking about this incident in Maine, of course."

"I supposed you were," Monteath said. "You're thorough, aren't you? Go back a long ways? And — far afield?"

"Probably," Bill said. "We've no way of knowing what's important, you know. About Maine?"

It had been, Monteath said, a ghastly business. He'd hoped to forget it; most of the time, he had forgotten it. He would admit that Wilmot's trick had — brought it back.

"Intentionally, you think?"

Monteath shrugged. He said, then, that he supposed so.

"At least," he said, "perhaps not the whole — er, prank. But my part in it. If that's true, it was a peculiarly — malicious thing to do." He paused. He had been looking away; he looked now at Bill Weigand. "Not a thing anyone would kill about," he said. "You're not getting that idea?"

"I shouldn't think it would be," Bill said. "Do you want to tell me more about this Maine incident, Mr. Monteath?"

"No," Monteath said. "I obviously don't. But I'm obviously going to, aren't I? Well — "

Monteath told briefly, almost dispassionately, as if it had happened to someone else, of the events long ago in Maine. He added nothing by his story to what Weigand had heard already. He described Joseph Parks.

"Obviously," Bill said, "he didn't resemble this mannequin of last night. Wilmot didn't try to carry it that far."

"Obviously," Monteath agreed. "The mannequin didn't resemble anybody I'd seen before. I said that."

"Yes," Weigand said. "I remember. So — after the party last night, you stopped by the Norths' apartment. Then?"

"Went downstairs, found a cab, went back to the Waldorf, went to bed. It was about two-fifteen when I took my watch off, put it on the night table. But if you're asking me to prove this — " He made a gesture. "How can I?" he said. "I had my room key with me. Even if I hadn't had — " He shrugged.

"No," Bill said. "But then, I haven't asked

you to, Mr. Monteath. Of course, if you happened to be able to identify the cab you took."

"Really, captain," Monteath said. "You don't expect that?"

"No," Bill said.

"I know nothing of Wilmot's death. I had no reason — no real reason — to kill him. But I'd say that in any case, of course."

"Of course," Bill agreed. "However — " He stood up. Monteath stood, too.

"I'm planning to take an afternoon train for Washington tomorrow," Monteath said. "That'll be all right?"

"Why yes," Bill said. "I don't see anything to prevent that, Mr. Monteath." He moved with Monteath toward the door. He said it was good of him to have come in. At the door, Bill said, "Oh, one more thing — " and Monteath stopped, waited.

"Had you met Baker before last night?" Bill asked. Monteath looked puzzled. He repeated the name.

"The man who was dressed as a child," Bill said. "In rompers, or something of the kind."

"Oh," Monteath said. "That was Baker? No, I don't remember ever meeting him. Damned embarrassing for him, the poor devil."

"Yes," Bill agreed. "It probably was. Annoying, probably. Embarrassing for the girl, too." He thanked Monteath again, closed the door after him. He stood for a moment, looking at the closed door.

"By the way, sergeant," he said, "see if they've got anything on the cab Mrs. Wilmot was supposed to take to Forest Hills, will you?"

Mullins used the telephone. There was nothing on the cab.

"Supposed to take?" Mullins said.

"Everything is supposition," Bill told him. "I suppose and you suppose and he and she suppose. Let's go see the Norths, sergeant."

"O.K., Loot," Mullins said. "I can sure use a drink."

Bill said he was surprised at Sergeant Mullins, but he did not sound particularly surprised.

VIII
Thursday, 6:10 P.M. *to* 7:20 P.M.

"You can always go by cats," Pamela North said. "Particularly Teeney. You should have seen them."

"Hissing?" Jerry said.

"Well, no. Not hissing, exactly. But they just took one look. Then they skedaddled. Teeney first. They simply hated him. And cats know."

She was asked to be reasonable; was told that cats — and particularly cats like Martini — are unpredictable; that the next time they met John Baker they might be all over him.

"Well," Pam said, "you just weren't here, that's all. They knew there was something about him, particularly Teeney. And she ran and of course the others ran too."

"She runs a good deal," Jerry said. "And when she does, the others do. She's the boss, you know. It's a case of 'Mom.' "

He was told he was merely pretending not to understand.

"No," Jerry said. "I'll grant that there's something, as you say, about Baker. From what you say. But I don't think cats can tell

183

murderers any better than anybody else, just by looking at them."

"They can smell them, probably," Pam pointed out. "Also, they've obviously got something else. Extra sensory. Anyway, I didn't say a murderer, necessarily. Just something. Something they didn't like."

"All we actually know," Jerry said, "is that they apparently love burglars. Remember?"

Pam did. It was a time the cats had not distinguished themselves. A sneak thief had broken into the Norths' apartment and had ransacked it, and there was every indication that the cats had followed him admiringly from room to room, ending with the bedroom, where the burglar had emptied Pam's box of jewelry onto a dresser and then — rather insultingly — taken none of it. When the burglar had departed, no doubt after kissing the cats goodbye, he had shut them in the bedroom. There is a theory that Siamese cats leap to the shoulders of intruders, holding them for the police.

"We don't know the burglar," Pam pointed out. "He was probably a very nice man, otherwise. You can always go by cats. And if they think there's something about Mr. Baker, I do too."

"Listen," Jerry said. "Baker admits he was at Wilmot's penthouse before anybody else this morning, and he doesn't say why. He as good as admits that he was following Art Monteath. He wasn't at his hotel when he said he was, and could have been off killing Wilmot. He pretends to be an ingenuous, almost half-baked youngster and you say he can be tough as nails. Obviously there's something. And then to prove it you — you fall back on the cats. Who don't like *any* strangers." He paused. "I'd be willing to bet," he added, "that they didn't warm up to your Miss Evitts, either."

"Oh," Pam said, "that was different. She was nervous and upset, and of course that affected them. Remember how Pete was when one of our guests stood on his head? I mean on his own head, not Pete's head. Pete thought — "

"Listen, Pam," Jerry said. "You mean to sit there, drinking a martini, and tell me Miss Evitts stood on her head? I mean — " He paused. "I'm damned if I know what I mean," he said.

Jerry North looked at his empty glass and shook his head thoughtfully. He arose, and Sherry spurted from his lap, and spoke of grief. Jerry moved toward the drink tray and the doorbell rang. "It'll be Bill," Pam said, and was proved right. It was also Mullins. Jerry moved on to the drink tray, making

185

more martinis; for Mullins, an old-fashioned. And Pam North told of Martha Evitts's distracted visit, of Baker's arrival, of his admissions and his changed demeanor, of his denial of murder which was, nevertheless, coupled with tacit approval of Wilmot's removal.

"Except," Pam said, "that he seemed to think it was premature. And, I was just telling Jerry, the cats don't like Mr. Baker. They think there's something."

"By the way," Bill Weigand said, looking around. "Where are all the cats?"

"Oh," Pam said, "they ran, probably. They usually do when — "

From his mixing tray, Jerry made a sound.

"Well," she said, "it was entirely different with Mr. Baker. But if you won't see, you — " She abandoned it. She told Bill Weigand that he ought to talk to Mr. Baker himself. She was told that that was planned, but that the well-known problem of catching the rabbit seemed to have arisen. "He's no rabbit," Pam said. "Not Mr. Baker. What hunts rabbits?" She considered. "Dogs," she said. "Cats. Owls, don't they? People. Mr. Baker is on that side."

"He admitted following Monteath?" Bill asked, and was told that he had, all but.

"But not," Bill said, "whether he caught up with Monteath? If he wanted to. Or — found out what he wanted to find out?"

Pam shook her head. She said, "Mr. Baker isn't what he appears to be, is he?" and waited.

"Apparently not," Bill said. He sipped from his glass. "Neither is Mr. Monteath, come to that," he said, and sipped again. "Mr. Monteath killed a man," he said, and got, *"Bill! No!"* from Pam.

"Not recently," Bill said. "Not here. Probably there's no connection but — coincidence. However, there is that. He shot, and killed, a man trying to break into a cottage he had."

He told them.

"The man had red hair!" Pam North said.

Bill smiled faintly, he shook his head.

"He *must* have had," Pam said. "Somebody's made a mistake."

That was possible, Bill agreed. He thought it very doubtful. The man — Joseph Parks — had been heavy-set, had had black hair. It was not a matter on which the records of the Maine state police would be likely to be in error.

"I don't understand it," Pam said. "It's all — wrong. Isn't it? Because red hair has to come into it."

"Or," Jerry said, "for red hair read red herring."

"Really, Jerry," Pam said. "Actually, the man Mr. Monteath killed — and you say nobody minded, Bill?"

187

"I suppose Parks minded," Bill said. "No — the police didn't 'mind.' At least, there was nothing to do. No charge to bring."

"This man, this Mr. Parks, was just the opposite of the dummy, wasn't he?" Pam said. "Heavy-set and the dummy was thin; black-haired and the dummy had red hair. I suppose there wasn't even the scar?"

They all looked at her, including Jerry.

"The scar?" Jerry said. "What scar?"

"You don't really see things, do you?" Pam said. "The dummy had a scar through one of his — its — eyebrows. It went through diagonally. The left eyebrow, I think and — "

"Wait," Bill said. He was sitting forward in his chair. "You're sure about that, Pam?"

"Of course," Pam said. "When I look at things I see them. You know that."

"A scar like this?" Bill said, and traced a line through his own left eyebrow with an index finger.

"A little more across," Pam said. "But — yes." She considered. "I thought I told about that before," she said.

"No," Bill said. "No. I wish you had, Pam. Because — I saw a man with a scar like that this afternoon."

"With red hair?" Pam said. "A thin man with red hair and the scar. A *live* dummy?"

"Not particularly thin," Bill said. "Gray

188

more than red. But a few years ago — yes, he might have resembled Mr. Wilmot's mannequin. And — he was going into Mr. Wilmot's store. Probably to see Mr. Wilmot's general manager. I did have a man follow him for a bit just on — well, I suppose because you make so much of the red hair, Pam. My man lost him." He smiled, faintly. "If I'd known about the scar, I might have used two men. I — "

He finished his drink, rather abruptly. Mullins, who had been sipping his, was startled, was aggrieved, by the decisiveness of the gesture. He raised his own glass quickly. Bill said, "Mullins, I think we'd better — " and the doorbell rang.

Jerry went to it. In the doorway there was a man of indeterminate appearance, backed by a tall policeman, who was by no means indeterminate.

"Look what I got, captain," the uniformed man said. "From the description it's — "

"Yes," Bill said. "It certainly is, isn't it? We've been looking for you, Mr. Frank. We've been looking all over."

"And here he is," the patrolman says, "here he is, calm as you please, like he owned it, trying to get into the Wilmot place." He jerked a thumb upward, indicating the penthouse. (It was rather, Pam thought, as if he

189

indicated Mr. Wilmot's present "place." If so, he took an optimistic view.) "Didn't even look around to see if maybe there was somebody watching. Didn't notice there was a seal across the door. Didn't — "

"Right," Bill said. "Thanks, Foster."

"The sergeant said you'd be here," Patrolman Foster said. "So I figured, I'll take this guy down to the captain and — "

"Right," Bill said. "You did a good job. I'll pass the word along. Meanwhile, you may as well get along back up."

"Yes sir," Foster said. He went.

"Now, Mr. Frank," Bill Weigand said.

"I'm sure, sir, I didn't realize you were looking for me," Sylvester Frank said. He spoke very nicely. "I certainly made no effort to avoid the police."

"No?" Bill said. "Nor to get in touch with them, did you?"

"Really, sir," Frank said. "I had no idea that I could be of any assistance — "

"Come off it," Bill said. "You were trying to get into the penthouse just now. What did you want there?"

"Some possessions of mine are in the apartment," Frank said. "When I read this afternoon of this very tragic event, sir, I — "

"This afternoon? You read of it this afternoon?"

Frank said, "Yes sir."

He was told that that was interesting. He was asked where he had been. "Since," Bill said, "you weren't at your room."

"Oh, no sir," Frank said. "That is, I was there, last night. Today I went to visit my mother. In Hoboken that is, sir. I try to see her at least once a week. She's quite old and not well and I'm all she has, sir."

He was told that that was very interesting. He was invited to continue.

"Thursday is my day off, sir," Frank said. "The usual day off. I generally visit my mother. She hasn't long to live, I'm afraid, and I try — "

"Right," Bill said. "You're a dutiful son. We're all touched. You visited your mother. Then, this afternoon, you learned that your employer had been murdered. Probably you were very upset?"

"Indeed yes, sir."

"So you came here — to Mr. Wilmot's apartment that is — and tried to get in to get these — what did you call them? — possessions?"

"That's quite true, sir. I have a key to the apartment, of course. It seemed — quite a proper thing to do, sir."

"There was a police seal on the door," Bill said. "I suppose you didn't notice that?"

191

"No sir," Frank said. "If I had, sir, I would not have attempted — "

He stopped because Weigand was emphatically shaking his head.

"It's no good, Frank," Bill said. "You were seen there this morning. Walking up the penthouse stairs. Don't you realize we check up on things, Frank?"

Frank hesitated. Then he changed.

"I'm afraid I didn't tell you all the truth, sir," Frank said. There was trepidation in his voice.

"No," Bill said. "You didn't, did you?"

"I'm afraid I — well, I hoped I hadn't been seen, sir," Frank said. "Joe — he's the elevator man, sir — "

"I know," Bill said.

"He wasn't in the car," Frank said. "He often isn't. People call him to do things, you know." He paused. "It's not really what I'd call a well-run building," he said, with disapproval. "So I ran the car up myself and — was it somebody on the top floor saw me, sir?"

Bill nodded. He waited.

"I saw nothing that will help, captain," Frank said. "I did go to visit my mother. And it is quite true that I wasn't trying to — to avoid the police. You'll believe that, sir?"

"No," Bill said, "I'm afraid not. You went

to the penthouse around ten this morning. A little after ten. You let yourself in. You saw your employer on the floor, dead. So — you went to visit your dear old mother in — "

"Hoboken, sir," Frank said. "I am very fond of my mother. I — I found it all very disconcerting, sir."

"And — went home to mama?"

Frank looked somewhat unhappy.

"I'm sure, sir," Frank said, "that I didn't intend — "

"Right," Bill said. "Let's say you didn't. You found Mr. Wilmot dead on the floor. Stabbed."

"It was a very shocking sight, sir."

"I'm sure it was," Bill said. "If you hadn't killed him yourself."

"Oh, no sir."

"So, when you'd recovered from your shock, you merely got out of there. Got the hell out of there. Went over to Hoboken and — told your mother about it? It didn't occur to you to mention that Mr. Wilmot was dead to anyone else?"

"It wasn't that at all, sir," Frank said. "I did try. I tried to call the police, sir. But the telephone seemed to be out of order."

He was told that that was very interesting. He was told that, after the instrument had been checked for fingerprints, the police had used it, and it had been in order. He was told, also, that there had been no fingerprints on the telephone.

"I'm afraid I can explain that, sir," Frank said. "After I tried to use the telephone — and I assure you it was out of order then — I — well, I wiped the instrument, sir. You see — "

"You didn't want anyone to know you'd been there," Bill said.

"I'm afraid I wasn't thinking very clearly," Frank said. "It was — rather an instinctive action, sir."

"All right," Bill said. "Get on with it."

Frank got on with it. Convinced that he could not telephone from the apartment — "sometimes telephones go out of order temporarily, sir" — he had left the apartment, using the fire stairs.

"Why — " Bill began, but then said, "Never mind. Go on, Mr. Frank."

He had never, Frank insisted, planned to let his discovery go unreported. Once on the street, he had gone in search of a telephone. He had found one in a cigar store a couple of blocks away, but, just as he was about to go into the booth, he had heard sirens. He had gone out of the store, without using the telephone, and partly retraced his steps — retraced them far enough to see one prowl car stopped and another stopping in front of the apartment building. He realized, then, that someone else had reported the murder.

"And went to Hoboken?"

"Yes sir. I'm afraid I did, sir. I suppose I should have gone to the police at once, sir, but — but — "

"You didn't want to. Do you usually avoid the police, Mr. Frank?"

"Oh no, sir. But it is natural not to wish to be — involved, sir."

Bill thought it over. Granting Frank's account probably was not true. Could he prove it untrue? Suppose Martha Evitts had gone to the apartment first. She had left it precipitately, had been seen by Pam North, and her appearance had startled Pam. But Pam had not gone directly to the penthouse. She had stopped first at her own apartment. Then she had gone to the top floor and made her discovery.

While Pam was in her apartment, Frank might have come to the building and ridden up to the penthouse. He might have found the body, made his abortive attempt to notify the police, taken his slow course downstairs, walked in search of a telephone. He might have been out of the penthouse by the time Pam — and the elevator operator, Joe — reached it. And Pam, moving quickly — and she did move quickly — might have got her call through to Weigand while Frank still plodded down the fire stairs. In that event, Frank might have heard sirens as he started to close the door of a telephone booth.

In other words, his version could not be proved untrue — at the moment.

"Right," Bill said. "We'll leave that for the moment. When did you leave the apartment — after the party, I mean?"

Frank had emptied ash trays, taken glasses and canapé trays to the kitchen; put what he could of the glasses in the electric dishwasher and turned it on. He had left the glasses in the washer, at Mr. Wilmot's suggestion. He thought it was a little before two o'clock when he left.

"Mr. Wilmot was having a nightcap," he said.

"Was he intoxicated?"

"Oh no, sir. That is — well, he'd been drinking, of course. But I certainly wouldn't say intoxicated, sir."

"Right," Bill said. "Then you went home? Didn't encounter anyone."

Frank hesitated. Then he said, "No one, sir."

(The hesitation seemed marked to Pam North. Surely Bill would pick it up.)

"Right," Bill said. "Now, there are one or

two points about the party, Frank. Things you might help clear up."

"Any way I can help, sir," Frank said. He was earnest.

"There's a thing that puzzles us," Bill said. "Perhaps you can help on that. You'd been with Wilmot for several years. Before he and Mrs. Wilmot were divorced?"

"For a few months, sir."

"The separation wasn't friendly?"

Again the hesitation.

"Well — no, sir. I'm afraid it wasn't. Mrs. Wilmot found Mr. Wilmot — trying. He was a great man for jokes, sir. Some of them Mrs. Wilmot didn't appreciate."

"Right," Bill said. "Yet — Mrs. Wilmot came to the party last night. Everything very amicable, I gather?"

"Oh yes, sir. Of course, it would be, with so many others present."

"Yes," Bill said. "What prevailed on her to come, do you suppose, Frank?"

"I suppose — " Frank began, innocence in his voice. But Bill Weigand looked at him. "Because she knew Mr. Parsons was going to be there," Frank said. "At least, I suspect that was the reason. Mr. Wilmot's nephew, you know."

"I know," Bill said.

"Mrs. Wilmot is very fond of Mr. Parsons,

captain," Frank said. "For all he's not related to her — not really related, I mean. I've always thought, sir, her not having any children, you know, and Mr. Parsons being a gentleman who — well, needed the maternal influence, sir. That she felt about him as she might have about a son, if I make things clear." He paused. "The maternal instinct is very strong, sir," he said.

Bill skipped that.

"She knew Mr. Parsons was going to be at the party?" he asked.

"Yes, sir. Mr. Wilmot told her on the telephone. I happened to overhear. I was occupied in the living room and Mr. Wilmot made no effort — "

"Right," Bill said. "You happened to overhear. Do you happen to remember words?"

"Not exactly, sir. But, generally, he was sure she would want to come because her 'dear Clyde' would be there. I do remember the 'dear Clyde,' sir."

"And you think that persuaded her?"

"Well, sir, she did come. Quite early, indeed."

"Right," Bill said. "Now about this mannequin. What do you know about that? The dummy Mr. Monteath shot?"

"Well," Frank said, "I helped rig it up. On wires, you know. So it would look natural on the terrace. Mr. Wilmot and I fastened wires to — "

"Never mind," Bill said. "I gather it looked natural?"

"Oh yes, sir."

"Where did it come from?"

"Mr. Wilmot brought it from the store, sir. He had it prepared there, I presume. It was in sections of course, sir. When he brought it, I mean."

"Right," Bill said. "You looked at it?"

"Yes, sir. When we were rigging it — "

"Right," Bill said. "You must have, of course. Did it remind you of anyone?"

Sylvester Frank gave facial evidence of surprise. "Remind me, sir?" he said. Bill nodded.

"Why no, sir," Frank said. "That is — it was just a dummy, sir. A mannequin, as you say. I'm afraid I don't quite understand what you mean, captain."

"Did it look like anybody, man?"

Frank contributed a moment of consideration. He shook his head.

"Red hair?" Bill said. "Thin face? Scar through the left eyebrow?"

"No sir," Frank said. "I don't think — " He broke off. "Mr. Barron has a slight scar," he said. "Mr. Albert Barron. It does — er — bisect one of his eyebrows. I believe the left, sir. But otherwise — Mr. Barron is quite gray, sir. And his face never struck me as thin, sir."

"Barron," Bill said. "Who is Mr. Barron?"

"He's the sales manager of the company," Frank said. "A very old friend of the late Mr. Wilmot, I believe. He was at the — er — gathering last night."

Bill looked at the Norths. Jerry shook his head. Pam said, "I don't know, Bill. I don't remember him particularly. But I don't remember a lot of them." She paused. "Names come and go," she said. "I don't remember anyone with a scar."

"It was not very evident," Frank said. "I assure you Mr. Barron was there."

"Has Mr. Barron irregular teeth?" Bill asked.

"Teeth, sir? I never noticed particularly, I'm afraid."

"B-a-r-o-n?" Mullins asked.

"Two 'R's' I believe, sir," Frank said. He was afraid he didn't know Mr. Barron's address.

"The point is," Bill said, "that this dummy didn't resemble Mr. Barron in other particulars? Aside from this scar?"

"No sir. The mannequin was a — that is, resembled a — much younger man, captain. I'm sure it was intended merely as a mannequin, sir."

"With red hair?" Pam North said.

Frank looked at her; he said he was sorry.

"Never mind," Pam said. "But it does come into it," she said, to Bill. "All right, Pam," Jerry said. "We know." "Please," Pam said, "don't be tolerant, darling."

Bill took Frank over the rest of the party, getting the account he had already got several times, if from a different angle, if in language nice to the point of the obsequious. He took Frank again to his departure from the penthouse a little before two that morning, with Mr. Wilmot remaining, alive, well and, it appeared, mildly thirsty. He took Frank down in the self-operated elevator to the street. He had, thereafter, seen no one whose presence in the neighborhood might be interesting?

The question was asked negligently.

But Frank, with words apparently already formed in his mind, about to reach his lips, hesitated.

"Well?" Bill said. "You did see someone?"

Frank hesitated further. But finally, with apparent reluctance, he nodded. He said that he was certain that it was nothing that would help Captain Weigand. "However it looks, sir. I'm certain that — "

"Right," Bill said. "I'll decide, Frank. Who did you see?"

"Mr. Parsons, sir. He was — "

Parsons had been coming down the street toward the entrance to the apartment building as Frank went out of it. Parsons had been, Frank thought, a little drunk. "In control of himself, sir. But — intoxicated, I'm afraid. He was earlier, sir." Parsons had turned into the apartment house. Frank had stopped to watch him; then Frank had gone on.

"When you saw him," Bill said, "he was wearing an overcoat? A topcoat?"

The question was simple enough. It appeared that the answer was not. There was a long pause before Frank spoke, and then he spoke with reluctance. "Yes," he said. "I'm — afraid so, captain. A gray topcoat."

"Afraid?" Bill said. "Why afraid, Frank?"

"Captain," Frank said, "I've been hoping I wouldn't have to say this. It's — it's been worrying me a great deal, sir. I — I hoped if I had time to think about it, I might — might see my way more clearly. But — " He stopped. He shook his head.

"All right," Bill said. "Let's have it, Frank."

"Mr. Parsons is such a fine young gentleman, sir," Frank said. "Things have been so — difficult for him. I hoped that I — wouldn't have to make them any more difficult. I'm sure there's an explanation, sir."

"Of what?" Bill said. "Get on with it."

"Mr. Parsons's coat — his topcoat, sir —

202

being in Mr. Wilmot's apartment," Frank said. "This morning after — after Mr. Wilmot was dead. Because I'm quite certain he was wearing the coat when I saw him before that and — and — "

"No," Bill said. "There wasn't any coat belonging to Mr. Parsons in the apartment. Not after the body was found. Try again, Frank."

Frank was sorry; it appeared he was hurt. He realized that he had given the captain cause not to trust him entirely but still — He would much have preferred not to mention it, as the captain must see. But —

"The coat was there," Frank said. "I'm afraid I took it when I left. It — it was lying on a sofa, sir. It had Mr. Parsons's name on a little label inside a pocket. So — I took it, sir. I was sure Mr. Parsons hadn't — done anything wrong — but, I could see how it might look, captain."

"You took the coat?"

Frank nodded.

"I — disposed of it," he said. "In a trash can on my way home, captain. I realize it was a — an unfortunate thing to do."

"Yes," Bill said. "It was — unfortunate, Frank." He looked at the indeterminate little man. "What kind of a damn fool are you?" he asked. "What's Parsons to you?"

"He was always very considerate, sir,"

Frank said. "I felt — "

"That you should be considerate in return," Bill Weigand said. "By destroying evidence. Making yourself an accessory. You realize that?"

"I'm very sorry, captain," Frank said. "I'm afraid I acted on an impulse."

"I suppose," Bill said, "the coat was covered with blood? Mr. Wilmot's blood?"

"Oh no, sir," Frank said. But as he spoke his eyes flickered away from Bill. It was momentary; then Frank looked again at Bill Weigand. "I do realize I was very wrong," he said. "I presume that now — that I — that I'm in trouble, captain?"

"Yes," Bill said, "you're in trouble, Mr. Frank." He paused. "One way or another," he said, "you're in quite a bit of trouble." He looked at Frank, who looked appropriately woebegone. "Sergeant," Bill said, "you'd better take Mr. Frank — " But he stopped. "No," he said. "Get Foster down here, will you, sergeant? We'll have him take Mr. Frank downtown."

Mullins went.

"I've told you everything that happened, captain," Frank said. "I don't know anything about what happened to Mr. Wilmot. I really don't, sir. You're going to — arrest me, sir?"

"I have, Mr. Frank," Bill said. "That is,

I'm holding you as a material witness."

"In jail, sir?"

"Right," Bill said. "In jail. After the district attorney's office has talked to you, and I've talked to you again, and a few more people, maybe you'll remember more. If you do, we'll see what happens next. But for the time being — " Weigand interrupted himself as Mullins came back. Mullins came alone.

"Nope," Mullins said. "No Foster, Loot."

"No relief?"

"Nobody," Mullins said. "Looks like a slip-up somewhere. Want I should get on to the precinct and — "

He stopped because Bill Weigand was shaking his head.

"No," Bill said. "I'll take care of it. You can take Mr. Frank downtown, book him as a material witness and then — I think you might take a little ride over to Long Island, sergeant. Don't you?"

"Yeah," Mullins said. "O.K., Loot. I see what you mean. Come on, you."

"You" was Sylvester Frank. He went. He still looked woebegone. But then, as he preceded Mullins through the door, as he may have thought Mullins's greater bulk shielded his face from the others, his expression of dejection was briefly replaced by another expression. His face was, for an instant, just visible to Pamela North. Pam could have sworn he smiled — almost smiled.

"Bill!" Pam said, as the door closed. "Bill. I think he planned the whole thing. Getting caught and everything. Even — Bill, *he was pleased at getting arrested!*"

The telephone rang. Jerry went to it.

"Because he must have known there'd be somebody," Pam said. "And all this business about *not* wanting to tell about Mr. Parsons's coat, and of denying there was blood on it so you wouldn't believe him and — "

"For you, Bill," Jerry said. "Stein."

" — pleased as Punch," Pam said. "And — "

"Yes, Pam," Bill said. "Yes, Stein? In a minute, Pam."

"Getting reports through on the fingerprints," Stein said. "From the Wilmot apartment. One of them is pretty interesting, captain. Remember Behren? Alexander Behren?"

"I'm not sure," Bill said. "Wait a minute."

"Yes," Stein said. "That's the one. The man who identified the man Monteath shot. Well, he was at the apartment recently, probably last night. Only — there's a catch in it." Stein paused for a moment. "Seems Behren's dead," Stein said.

"That," Bill said, "is quite a catch. Go

206

ahead, sergeant."

Stein went ahead. The many prints set and photographed in the Wilmot penthouse were being processed. So far, only two prints of particular interest had shown up — the man who had left a print inside the safe had touched other objects in the apartment. For one thing he had been at the files. And, a second set of prints, coded to Washington in accordance with routine, proved to belong to one Alexander Behren. The army had turned the prints up. Behren had been drafted late in 1942, at the age of twenty-nine. He had been — "listen to this, captain" — five feet ten inches tall. He had weighed one hundred and thirty-eight pounds. He had had red hair. He had had, as a distinguishing mark, a scar through his left eyebrow. "Apparently," Stein said, "he ran into something sharp a good while ago. Or somebody took a knife to him."

Behren had gone through training. He had been sent to the Pacific. He had been in the New Guinea fighting. And there he had vanished. "Missing, believed dead." He had remained missing, was still believed dead. His body had never been identified; a good many had never been. But, dead or alive, he had attended Mr. Wilmot's last party. "In a way," Stein said, "it looks as if he attended it twice, doesn't it, captain?"

"Yes," Bill said, "in a way it does. Anything else?"

There was nothing else. Martha Evitts was still missing. John Baker was still missing. Sylvester Frank was still —

"No," Bill said. "Not Frank any more. You can call them off on Frank." He explained, briefly. He replaced the receiver. He looked at Pam and Jerry North, who waited.

"A man named Behren," Bill told them. "It seems he was at the party last night. It seems that he — "

"But the butler told us that," Pam said. "He said Mr. Barron was there. The man with the scar."

"No," Bill said. "This man's name is Behren." He spelled it. "Alexander — " He stopped. Albert Barron. Alexander Behren.

"Well," Bill Weigand said, "I'll be damned if he didn't."

"The red-haired man," Pam said. "It has to be, Bill. Red hair turned to gray hair!" She turned to Jerry. "Red herring indeed," Pam North said. "I told you — "

"Right," Bill said. "You did. And — Mr. Behren, who's supposed to be dead, identified the man Monteath killed in Maine." He continued to look at the Norths. He smiled faintly.

"Everything clear now?" he asked.

IX

Thursday, 7:20 P.M. *to* 9:35 P.M.

Martha Evitts raised her cup to her lips. But she put it down, the coffee untasted. She looked at John Baker, across from her at a small table in a small restaurant near Times Square.

"What it comes down to," she said, "is that you're not what I thought you were. Are you?"

"Yes," he said. "In what matters to us."

She shook her head.

"Different," she said. "Completely different." She paused. "Older," she said. "For one thing — older."

"As a matter of fact, yes," he said. "But that's all right, isn't it?"

"Oh," she said. "That's all right. But it doesn't matter much, does it?"

"I'm the same man," he said. "As far as we're concerned, exactly the same man. I wish you'd believe that."

"Oh," she said. "I try. I try to believe so many things. You — you don't help me much, John."

"All I can," he said. "All I can right now.

209

I'm sorry it's that way, but it is."

"You're mixed up in something."

He said she could call it that. He drank coffee.

"Again," he said. "I had nothing to do with killing Wilmot. I don't know who did. I was there — at the penthouse — about something else. I expected to find Wilmot alive. Leave him alive."

"You followed this man — what's his name? Monteath. Mrs. North saw you. You didn't deny it."

"No," he said. "I didn't. I don't. And — I can't tell you any more about it."

He was told he asked a lot.

"All right," he said. "I ask a lot, Martha. But, I didn't kill Wilmot. I didn't want him dead."

"You could," she said, "tell me anything. I wouldn't be — upset. It'd be better than the way it is."

"There's nothing I can tell you," he said. "Not now."

"Nor," she said, "tell the police?"

"Nothing that would help," he said. "Probably nothing they don't suspect, anyway. Or will get on to before long. You'll just have to believe that — well, that things will be all right."

"I'm trying," the girl said. "I'm trying very hard, John."

"Then," he said, "drink your coffee." He looked at his watch. "I've got to make a telephone call," he said. "Wait for me. Then I'll take you home. Sit here and drink your coffee and — quit worrying."

"That's fine," Martha said. "That's wonderful."

"You'll wait?"

"Yes, I'll wait. I'll drink my coffee."

He looked across the table at her. He smiled suddenly, and his face changed. He's the other John, now, she thought. She said, "I'll wait."

He still hesitated, but only for a moment. He went between tables to a telephone booth near the restaurant entrance. He dialed a number. When he was answered he said, "This is Baker." Then he listened.

"Yes," he said, "I'd think so. He went there."

He listened again.

"How important is it?" he asked, and again listened. He said, "I suppose he could" and listened again.

"It forces our hand," he said. "But, if it's forced, it's forced. When?"

As he listened, he whistled. He said it didn't give much time. He said, "O.K., I see what you mean." He hung up the receiver and went back to the table. He looked at Martha Evitts's cup. He said, "You didn't drink it all."

"Almost," she said.

"Martha," he said. "I can't take you home after all. There's something I've got to do. Will you go home?"

"Yes," she said. "I may as well."

"And stay there?"

"Yes."

"The police may show up," he said. "Tell them what you know, if you need to. They'll know it by now from these Norths of yours, anyway. Tell them you don't know where I am." He smiled faintly. "By then you won't," he said. "All right?"

"I guess so. I guess it has to be."

"For a while," he said. "You ready now?"

She was. They walked together to the Times Square station of the IRT. She went toward the uptown express platform.

"I go the other way," he told her. "Stay at home?" She nodded. "Don't worry," he said. She smiled. It was not a particularly good smile.

John Baker went to the other express platform. He took a downtown train. He was still on it when it tilted down into the tunnel beneath the East River.

Acting Captain William Weigand sat at his desk. He ate a hamburger on a roll and drank coffee. The coffee tasted of cardboard container; the hamburger tasted of nothing in particular. Weigand used the telephone. His voice traveled some hundreds of miles and was heard by a uniformed state police officer in a barracks in Maine.

"I appreciate it was a long time ago," Bill said. "I realize you've looked it up once for Sergeant Stein. It looks like meaning more now." He listened. "Right," he said. "I'll wait."

He held the telephone in one hand and the hamburger in the other, eating because, with no time for a proper dinner, one has to eat. He felt the beginning of that sense of urgency which so often came when, finally, a case began to take shape. But logic lagged behind; what he had hold of remained, to the mind, amorphous. More accurately, Bill thought, he seemed to have a case in either hand, as in one hand he held a telephone receiver and in the other a hamburger on a bun. He waited for a man in Maine to consult records of years ago.

"All right," the man in Maine said, "I've got what there is. It isn't much. This man Monteath, summer resident, killed a man he says tried to break in. The man was identified as Joseph Parks by a man who said he was a friend of his. Fingerprints checked. Small-time crook from your town."

"No charges against Monteath?"

"Nope."

"No suspicion there was any funny business?"

"Not on the record," a twanging voice from Maine said. "I wasn't on the case. The man who was on it got himself shot five-six years ago. If he had any suspicions they don't show on what we've got."

"Right," Bill said. "I'm interested in this man who identified Parks. Alexander Behren, we have it."

"That's the name we've got here," Maine said.

"How did Behren happen to show up?" Bill asked. "Read about an unidentified man being shot? I suppose he was unidentified until Behren showed up? No papers on him."

"Seems not," Maine said. "Hold it."

Bill held it, this time briefly.

"Behren showed up the next morning," Maine said. "Guess he didn't read about it, because how could he? Wasn't printed yet. Seems he reported a friend of his had been going to meet him somewhere and hadn't. Described the friend, and it fitted. Looked at Parks, and sure enough."

"Right," Bill said. "He could have known when he showed up what he would find?"

"Well," Maine said, in the accents of Maine, "he could have. Said he didn't, apparently."

"Do you know whether he had any contact

with Monteath? Behren, I mean. After he turned up?"

"Nothing to show. Wait a minute. Probably didn't. Monteath's wife was in a hospital down in Portland. Pretty sick, seems like. Monteath wanted to get there, and apparently the boys let him. Pretty early in the morning he left."

"You've got the name of the hospital?"

The state police office had. He gave it to Weigand.

"One more thing," Bill said. "I don't suppose your record gives a description of Behren?"

There was a brief pause.

"Nope," Maine said. "No reason it should, is there?"

"None," Bill said. He thanked Maine. He depressed the buttons on the telephone set, released them. He wanted somebody in authority — a resident would do, a telephone operator would not — at a hospital in Portland. He replaced the receiver and spent some minutes in thought, which produced little save more questions. Had there, for example, really been blood on Clyde Parsons's topcoat? Had the coat really been in the penthouse at all? Sylvester Frank was a liar. But, how much had he lied? The telephone rang.

"Got a doctor up there," the police operator said. "He do?"

"Put him on," Bill said. "We'll have to find out." He waited. A distant voice said, "Hello? Dr. Farley speaking."

Weigand identified himself. He said he was interested in finding out what he could about a Mrs. Arthur Monteath, who had died in the hospital late in July of 1940. Could Dr. Farley help him? Or put him on to someone who could?

"I doubt it," Farley said. "I can't, anyway. Not here then. I can try records, but there may not be anybody there. It's late here."

"I know," Bill said. "It's late here too, doctor. See if you can get me switched, will you?"

It took time. A faint sound indicated that a bell might be ringing somewhere in a distant hospital. Then the ringing stopped. Then Weigand was asked what number he was calling. But then a voice said, faintly, "Records." "I'm ringing your party," another operator said, and Bill Weigand said, "Please. This is police business. Stay out, will you?"

"You rang," Records said, distantly. "I'm sor-*ree*," an operator said, elaborately. "Excuse it please."

"Is this the records room?" Bill said, raising his voice above confusion. "There's no need to shout," Records said.

Bill was sorry, or sor-ree. He explained.

"Really!" Records said. Records was young,

female. "All those years ago?" The years might have constituted a lifetime; Bill supposed, from the voice, that in this case they constituted the major part of one.

"It's important," Bill said. "Police business. I'm calling from New York."

"Well," Records said. "I'll look." A distant madman was to be humored. "What was the name again?"

Bill gave it and waited. He did not wait long. Mrs. Arthur Monteath had been admitted to the hospital on July 27, 1940. Myocardial infarction. She had died on July 29, after a second heart attack. Body had been claimed by her husband.

It was what Bill had expected. It was all there was to it — a young woman, recently married, on vacation with her husband in a little cottage near the sea, where the beat of water against rocks was never silent, had had a heart attack and two days later had died of it, or of another. There was no point in carrying it further.

"Can you give me the name of the doctor?" he asked. "Of the nurse? Is either of them there now?"

Records could. The doctor had, she thought, left Portland. The nurse — "Oh," Records said. "That's Aunty." Records gasped slightly. "I'm sorry," she said. "The night superin-

217

tendent of nurses, now. Yes — I suppose she's here. But I'm afraid she'll be too busy to — "

"Try," Bill told her. "Give me her name and try."

Ten minutes later, Bill Weigand put the telephone receiver in its cradle and sat looking at it. The warm friendliness of a middle-aged voice was still in his ears. If he were in a hospital, he would like to have Alice Blanchard as his nurse. "The poor, poor thing," she had said, of Grace Monteath. "She was so young, really. It was so sad her — her not wanting to live. I've thought of her so often, wondered so often."

Bill wondered now.

Grace Monteath had had a heart attack; a serious enough attack, but no more serious than many people had and recovered from, and lived for years after. She had been brought to the hospital by her husband on a summer morning. She had been put to bed — given digitalis, and oxygen and anti-coagulant drugs. And, the prognosis had been favorable. She had not gone into shock; there was every prospect that, with a few weeks of rest and treatment, she would recover sufficiently to lead an almost normal life. They told her that, and she did not seem to hear them.

The doctor had been able to reassure Monteath, to tell him there was no immediate danger. He had driven back to the cottage "to get their things, you know" and had returned the next day, quite early. He had seen his wife briefly, with the nurse present. Grace Monteath had seemed cheerful enough, then. She had said, "Of course I'll be all right, darling."

"I remember how she said that," Nurse Blanchard said. "It was for him, really."

Monteath had said nothing about what had happened at the cottage earlier that morning; of that Nurse Blanchard was sure. He had not stayed long; the doctor would not let him stay long. Later in the day they had heard at the hospital of the shooting, and had cautioned Monteath not to mention it. He had said that he knew better than to do that, and he had not when he visited his wife again that afternoon. "He spent most of the day at the hospital," Nurse Blanchard said. "He was terribly upset, of course."

By then, Nurse Blanchard had begun to suspect Grace Monteath did not want to live. "She just lay there, waiting to die." The nurse could not understand it. "She had so much to live for, and she loved him so much, and he loved her so much."

Mrs. Monteath had fallen into a light sleep the evening of the day after her attack, and she had talked in her sleep. She had said, "I've spoiled it all. Spoiled everything" and "I didn't mean to, Art. I didn't — " Her voice had trailed off, then. But, a few minutes later, she had spoken again, this time excitedly. "Don't try to do anything," she had said. "There's nothing anybody can do. Not anybody, Art. I've spoiled it all." She had had morphine to quieten her; had been quiet through the night.

But when she wakened the next morning, Grace Monteath had lain with her eyes wide, staring up at the ceiling. She had not wanted food, not wanted anything.

Nurse Blanchard, on duty again, had been disturbed by her patient's condition, although physically there had been no change — had been nothing to change the originally hopeful prognosis. When it was almost time for the doctor to make his morning calls, Nurse Blanchard had gone to the door to watch for him, to ask him to see Mrs. Monteath before the others. She had stood in the open door, looking down the corridor, and then had heard the sound behind her.

Mrs. Monteath had thrown off the covers, the oxygen tent. She had thrown herself out of bed, violently; she had stood and then —

"It was as if she was trying to dance," Nurse Blanchard said. "It was — the last thing she should have done, of course. If she had wanted to live."

It had, quite literally, been the last thing Grace Monteath had done. She had cried out in her strange dance and collapsed while the nurse was still crossing the room toward her. She had died a few minutes later of a second attack.

"Which she wanted to happen," the nurse said. "Which she made happen."

"She couldn't have been sure," Bill Weigand said. "Even violent exercise might not have killed her."

"No," Nurse Blanchard said. "But — it did. And, she wanted it to."

Monteath had not been told of the circumstances of his wife's death — not by Nurse Blanchard certainly; she was almost sure not by the physician. He had been let believe she had died peacefully, after a second attack which, while it had not been thought probable, had always been a possibility.

"What good would it have done to tell him?" Nurse Blanchard asked.

"None," Bill said. "You're quite certain she hadn't heard of this business at the cottage. The shooting of this man?"

"I'm as sure as I can be," Nurse Blanchard said. "Nothing that would worry her. We always try to avoid that."

221

Weigand looked at the telephone and did not see it. In effect, Grace Monteath had killed herself because she no longer wanted to live. Because she had "spoiled" something, "spoiled everything." And someone — almost certainly her husband — was not to try to do anything, because there was nothing that could be done.

And somehow, Bill told himself, that is linked with this. It was irrational to decide so; there was no evidence to support the decision. But Bill knew there was a link. Call it a hunch. Call it that strange, urgent tightening of the nerves. It was linked by Monteath himself. By a man named Behren. Or, now, a man named Barron — Albert Barron.

Bill consulted a telephone book. There was half a column of Barrons, including several Alberts. He used the telephone. The Albert Barron who was associated, as sales manager, with Wilmot's Emporium, lived in Mount Kisco. He had a telephone number, and Bill asked for it. For a long time a telephone rang somewhere in Mount Kisco, and was not answered. Bill hung up while it was still ringing.

He drummed with fingers on the surface of his desk. He took up the telephone again, got another number from the files. Mr. Bertram Dewsnap lived in the Flatbush section of Brooklyn which seemed, at the moment, almost as far as Mount Kisco.

Bill called Mr. Dewsnap. This time the telephone was answered. Mr. Dewsnap was anxious, as always, to be of help. No, he had no plans for the evening. He would be at home. If Captain Weigand wanted to come, to ask about this new thing which had come up, Mr. Dewsnap would be waiting to give what help he could. He couldn't imagine what it would be, but still —

Bill went down to his car. He drove toward Brooklyn.

There were lights in almost all the comfortable houses, set back with decent reserve on either side of the comfortable street in Forest Hills. Cars stood against the curb in front of some of the houses, and in the driveways of others — sensible, family cars; cars for shopping, for driving to the station, for unhurried vacation trips in the summer. Parked in front of the home of Mrs. Gertrude Wilmot, Mul-lins's car looked like any of the others. Mullins himself, getting out, might have been, in the gentle light which came from widely distributed street lamps, which came, too, from the houses themselves, any husband and father coming home, a little late — "some things came up at the last minute, mother" — from any office in the city.

Sergeant Mullins stood for a moment beside

the small sedan and looked up and down the street. Some of the people had gone to the early show; they had left lights on in entrance halls. Sergeant Mullins counted the number of houses which, were he a burglar, he would be reasonably sure he could enter safely — houses where lights in entrance halls, and not elsewhere, said, "We've all gone to the movies. Come and get whatever we have." Sergeant Mullins walked up the cement path, and up wooden steps, to the porch of Mrs. Gertrude Wilmot's home. He pressed the doorbell. Inside a bell shrilled.

A radio, or television, sounded in the house. Perhaps Mrs. Wilmot, living others' lives, laughing others' laughter, had not heard the bell. Mullins pressed again, this time, automatically, twice in quick succession. The sound stopped inside; the porch light went on; after a moment the door opened and Mrs. Gertrude Wilmot, plump and comfortable, looked up at Mullins from blue eyes and said, "Oh, you're one of the policemen, aren't you?"

"Yes ma'm," Mullins said. "There're one or two points, Mrs. Wilmot."

"Come in," Mrs. Wilmot said. "Do come in, Mr. — ?" Mullins told her his name, he went in. The chintz living room was bright; silk-shaded lamps, a pair of them with fringe, were warm centers of light. It was a very pretty room, Sergeant Mullins thought. He would not have supposed, however, that Mrs. Gertrude Wilmot smoked a pipe. Mullins did not permit himself to appear to sniff.

"I do hope I can help," Mrs. Wilmot said.

"The captain wonders — " Mullins said.

"Please sit down, sergeant," Mrs. Wilmot said. "I wonder if I couldn't get you a cup of coffee?"

"I guess not, ma'm," Mullins said. "The captain wonders whether you can't give us a little more complete description of this cab you took last night. This morning, rather. The one you took home?"

"Oh dear," Mrs. Wilmot said. "I'm so afraid I can't, sergeant. I didn't notice. It was — it was just a taxicab. And the driver didn't say much. I always mean to look at the picture and make sure that the driver is really the right man, but somehow I never do."

"No ma'm," Mullins said. "Nobody does much. Still — " He paused. "You see," he said, "they like us to get all the loose ends tied up. You see what I mean, Mrs. Wilmot? What people call shipshape. We haven't been able to find the driver of the cab you took. We'd like to take a look at his trip record sheet, so we wouldn't have to bother you anymore."

"So you'd know I really did take a cab," she said. "Didn't just say I did, but really go back and kill my former husband?"

"Nobody says that," Mullins told her. "We — well, we just want it made certain you couldn't of." Mullins paused. A familiar voice was in his remembering ears. "Couldn't have," Mullins said, with care. "But, if you don't recall, you don't."

She was, she said, terribly sorry.

"You came out here just for that?" she asked.

Sometimes, Mullins told her, they had to go a long way for very little. Just to get one fact for the record — or to try to get it.

"All the way out for nothing," she said. "I'm so sorry. Can't I at least give you a cup of coffee? Or even something a little stronger?"

It was very nice of her, but no. Mullins then appeared to remember something else.

"There's one other point," he said. "Have you seen your nephew — Mr. Parsons, that is — today?"

Her face clouded. She shook her head.

"I did so hope he'd call me up," she said. "But — nothing. I'm so worried he's — well, you know — I — "

"There're one or two points the captain thinks he might help clear up," Mullins said. He spoke a little more loudly than was entirely necessary; it was as if he had rather suddenly come to the conclusion that Mrs. Wilmot was deaf. "One's about a topcoat." The last was louder than ever. Then Mullins said, "Come now, Mrs. Wilmot. Don't tell me you smoke a pipe."

"No," Clyde Parsons said. He stood in a doorway which led from the living room to a room behind it. "No. She couldn't very well get you to believe that, could she? Not Aunt Trudie." He put a hand on the frame of the doorway. "Not that she wouldn't try," he said. "She'd try damn near anything, bless her."

"Oh Clyde!" Mrs. Wilmot said. "I'm so *sorry,* Clyde."

"We were foolish to try it," Parsons said. "Doesn't look so good, now we didn't get away with it. Does it, sergeant?"

"No," Mullins said. "It wasn't very bright, Mr. Parsons. If it had been a cigarette, now, it would have been — " He broke off and regarded Mrs. Wilmot. "Even that wouldn't have been so good," he said. "What was the idea, Mr. Parsons?"

"Not that I know anything I haven't told you," Parsons said. He came into the room. He was very pale; his hand shook a little as he took his pipe out of his pocket and put it between his teeth. "I just couldn't see any point in going over it again."

"He's not well," Mrs. Wilmot said. "He's in no condition to be — "

"Now, Trudie," Clyde Parsons said, and his voice was gentle.

"Well, you're not," she said. "You need a good rest and — "

"I," Parsons said, "have got one of the world's fanciest hangovers. I've got the shakes. The sergeant can see what's the matter with me, Trudie. My head's in pieces. I need a drink. I'm not taking one."

"Oh dear," Mrs. Wilmot said. "Perhaps under the circumstances you ought — "

"No," Parsons said. "I guess I won't, Trudie. Well, sergeant, what's this about a topcoat?"

"You lost yours last night," Mullins told him. "It might be important where you lost it."

"I don't know," Parsons said. He sat down, rather slowly, a little carefully. "That is — yes, I seem to have lost it. I don't know where. This morning when I woke up, it wasn't around. That's all I know." He nodded. "Believe it or not," he said. "That's all I know about it. I pulled a blank — a complete blank."

"You didn't have it when you got home about four this morning," Mullins said. "But — we hear your coat was found, later, in Mr. Wilmot's apartment."

Parsons looked quickly at Gertrude Wilmot. He looked away, again at Mullins.

"I gotta tell you, I guess," Mullins said. "You don't have to answer anything without a lawyer, if you want one."

Parsons shook his head.

"I can't answer," he said. "A lawyer wouldn't help. I don't know, sergeant. That is — "

"But," Gertrude Wilmot said, "*I* know, Clyde. And I'm going to tell the sergeant. Because there isn't anything to hide and we — we don't *need* a lawyer."

It was rather more than Mullins had bargained for. That, if the relationship between Clyde Parsons and his aunt was as close as Frank had indicated, he might well go to her had been obvious. That he would wait there, smoking a pipe to make his presence known, until the police arrived, was possible, but not to be expected. That now Mrs. Wilmot was "going to tell the sergeant" was something the sergeant had not anticipated. But of course, Mullins thought, if the nice little lady was going to tell too much it might help and — they couldn't hold her to it. Not with only Mullins to hear.

"O.K.," Mullins said. "But you don't have to say anything without a lawyer."

"I know," Mrs. Wilmot said. "Well — I didn't come straight home from the party, sergeant. I — "

She had, she said, tried to get Clyde into a cab with her, planning to bring him home to Forest Hills. That was true enough. He had wrenched away; that, also, was true. But, Mrs. Wilmot had not given up so readily.

She had followed him, in the cab. In the cab, she had waited outside barrooms. Once, when he had been in one bar for some time, she had started to go in and look for him, but by then he was coming out. He had been very drunk; apparently he had not even seen her.

Mullins looked at Parsons, who shook his head slowly.

"I don't remember any of this," he said. "But — it's the sort of thing Trudie would do."

"Anybody would do it," she said, and went on.

She had kept the cab. "Of course, I had to make it worth the man's while." From the last bar, Parsons had gone toward the apartment house where his uncle lived.

"Wait a minute," Mullins said. "Did he have a coat on? A topcoat?"

"Of course not," Mrs. Wilmot said. "I thought I told you that. Such a chilly night and I was afraid — well, that he'd just lie down somewhere and — "

Parsons groaned slightly.

But Parsons had not lain down somewhere, there to acquire pneumonia. He had gone, not steadily but persistently enough, back to the apartment house. Mrs. Wilmot had trailed him, seen him go in.

"There was another man there," Mullins said. "Anyway, he says he was. Your hus — Mr. Wilmot's butler."

"Sylvester," Mrs. Wilmot said. "Was he? I didn't see him."

That made it even, if Frank had told the truth. And if Mrs. Wilmot was telling it. They might both be; Frank might easily not have noticed a cab, following a little way behind a walking man, when his eyes were on the man.

When her nephew had gone into the apartment house, Mrs. Wilmot had paid off the cab driver, and gone in after him. She did not say why she did this; it was not necessary for her to say why. By the time she had reached the lobby it was empty. The elevator door was closed and she could hear the sound of the car's movement in the shaft. At first she thought the elevator had stopped at the fifth floor, since the indicator which should have marked its progress pointed there. But then she noticed that the indicator did not move, although the car, from the sound, still

231

did. She was certain Clyde Parsons was in the elevator, and certain she knew where he was going.

"I knew he wouldn't do anything," Mrs. Wilmot said. "But — Byron had been so mean to him and — "

"You can never tell what a drunk will do," Clyde Parsons said from his chair. "There's no accounting for drunks."

"Clyde," Gertrude Wilmot said. "I *do* know. Anyway, what you wouldn't do."

Clyde Parsons had been holding his head in both hands. He lowered his hands for a moment and smiled, a little crookedly. He put his hands back. He'd really tied one on, Sergeant Mullins thought, with sympathy.

Mrs. Wilmot had pressed the button to bring the elevator down. After some time, it came. She got into it and went up to the top floor, climbed the stairs toward the penthouse.

She met her husband's nephew coming down the stairs.

"Won't let me in," Clyde said. "Want to get my coat and the old — " Mrs. Wilmot paused in her quotation, and evidently chose a word. "The old gentleman won't let me in. Says I didn't leave any coat. S'drunk, that's what he is."

He might have been, Mullins thought. That fitted. On the other hand, the intoxicated notoriously see drunkenness around them. On another hand, there might be no truth in any of it.

"You left with Mr. Parsons," Mullins said. "When you left the party, I mean. Did he have a topcoat then?"

"No," Mrs. Wilmot said, quickly. "He didn't. I remember thinking he ought to have."

"Another thing," Mullins said, "you went up immediately after Mr. Parsons?"

"As soon as the elevator took him up and came down again."

"Yeah," Mullins said. "How long would you figure that was, Mrs. Wilmot?"

She paused, seemed to reckon.

"A minute or two," she said.

Mullins also reckoned. "A minute or two" was obviously an underestimate. But even if one made it five minutes, over all, Parsons could hardly have been more than three minutes on the top floor and above, since part of her waiting time he would have spent in transit. It didn't look like being long enough — if she was telling the truth.

And it did explain the presence of the topcoat in the penthouse apartment, assuming Sylvester Frank had actually found it there.

"You don't remember any of this, Mr. Parsons?" Mullins said.

Parsons uncovered his face. He said "No." He shut out the light again with protecting hands.

"O.K.," Mullins said. "Then what?"

Then, Mrs. Wilmot said, she and Parsons had gone down again. Outside the apartment house, she had again tried to persuade him to go home with her. But again he had wrenched away and gone off, and this time there was no convenient cab to help her. She had tried to follow him but, although his progress had not been steady, it had been rapid. She had lost him within a block or two. Only then — only some minutes after she had realized he had disappeared in the night, in the tangled streets of the Washington Square area — did she find a cab driver willing to make the long trip to Forest Hills.

"And I don't remember anything about the cab, I'm afraid," she told Mullins.

It had come full circle; they still needed to find a taxicab which had made a trip. If one had, they would find it in the end.

Mullins considered. He looked at his watch, found that the time was almost eight-thirty. Parsons and Mrs. Wilmot would have to be talked to further; the captain would want to talk to them; the assistant district attorney of the Homicide Bureau would want to talk to them. But it was late, with no more than they had — with, specifically, no wedge of fact with which to crack the story — to take them in. Material witnesses or not, Mullins decided, they might as well spend the night in the comfortable house.

"The Loot — I mean the captain — will want to talk to you," he told them both. "A lot of other people will. I could take you in and have you both booked as material witnesses. If I don't, will we find you here tomorrow?"

"Of course," Mrs. Wilmot said. Mullins waited. "Sure," Parsons said.

Mullins did not precisely leave it at that, although he left Mrs. Wilmot and Parsons in the comfortable house, in the chintz living room. Back in the police car, he used the car's radio telephone. The local precinct would provide a man to cover the Wilmot house for the night, to see that the birds remained nested. "Two men would be better," Mullins said, "front and rear." He was told that, if he wanted to be that sure, he had better take his people in.

"O.K.," Mullins said. "One man, then."

He drove back to Manhattan, stopping at a diner.

Weigand was not at the office of Homicide West. He expected to be back shortly; Mullins was to wait. Mrs. North had called, asking for the captain, then for Mullins.

"And," the detective on duty said, "there's another thing. This man Frank you took in. He's out again. Lawyer showed up with a writ."

Things like that were to be expected. "O.K.," Mullins said. "We'll get him when we want him."

"They say Frank seemed sort of surprised," the detective said.

X

Thursday, 8:55 P.M. *to* 10:18 P.M.

It is absurd for a captain of detectives, Police Department, City of New York — even an acting captain — to get himself lost in the City of New York — even in the Borough of Brooklyn. It is true that Brooklyn, once the area around Borough Hall is uneasily ventured from, is a labyrinth for Manhattanites, best traversed with a lifeline trailing out behind. It is true that duty infrequently takes Acting Captain William Weigand across the East River, and that pleasure takes him there hardly more often, and then by the most direct route to Ebbets Field. It is nevertheless ridiculous for a police officer to get lost in his own city.

Against the realization that he was lost, Bill fought a dogged, rear-guard, action. It was not until he discovered that he had once more, and for the third time, got himself on what was too evidently the wrong side of Prospect Park that he decided to ask a policeman. It was some time before he found one, and he approached with the hope that he would not be recognized. After all, convertible

237

Buicks are not standard equipment in the police department; Bill's was his own, operated by dispensation — and at considerable saving to the department. Of course, there was the matter of the auxiliary red headlights —

"Yes sir," the patrolman said, and saluted. "What can I do for you, inspector?"

Patrolmen are expected to be observant. This one was, in addition, tactful — a policeman in plain clothes, in a Buick Roadmaster, might be expected to be an inspector. (Cadillac, chief inspector.)

Bill identified himself. He supplied the address he sought. It was something of a relief that the patrolman had to look it up in a small book; that, having found the name of the street, he looked at it with mild reproach.

"Can't say I blame you, captain," he said. "Well — first thing, you get back to Flatbush Avenue. Then — "

Bill listened, and remembered. He gave thanks, U-turned, and followed directions. It was nevertheless almost nine-thirty when he stopped in front of a house — detached certainly, but rubbing shoulders with houses on either side — in a narrow street. The house was unlighted, so far as he could see from the curb. Mr. Dewsnap did not welcome with illumination.

Bill left the car and walked up to the glass-paneled door and pushed a doorbell button. There was no answering sound. He raised his hand to knock and lowered the fisted hand.

There was a light inside — a thin, hard pencil of light, sharply white. It moved this way and that, questingly, in a room to the right of the entrance hall. It was a furtive light, stealing about the room.

Bill Weigand raised his hand again and now knocked sharply on the door. The little light went out. There was no sound from inside.

Bill Weigand knocked again, and waited. He stood close to the door, with an ear to the glass panel. Faintly, now, he heard movement in the house. The sound was surreptitious, as the light had been.

Bill tried the door, and the knob turned. He tried to open the door quietly, but it stuck in the frame and, when pressure released it, it opened with a sharp, protesting sound. Then, in the dark house, Bill heard the footsteps of a hurrying man. Bill started toward the sound and ran into a chair and the chair toppled to bare floor. The crash of the chair on wood drowned out any other sound, if there was any other sound. Bill swore softly, and reached for a cigarette lighter. But he paused; there was no good reason for getting himself shot.

He groped along the wall, and found a doorway leading to his right. He felt along the wall near the door jamb and, after exasperating delay, found what he was after. He pressed the tumbler of the light switch and, as light came on, swung to flatten himself against the wall. And then he felt somewhat foolish in a bare entrance hall, empty of adversary — empty of almost everything; furnished only by a small table, with a telephone on it.

Then he heard the sounds again, and they came from the rear of the house.

"Dewsnap?" Bill called, and waited and got no answer. But then he heard another door being opened, somewhere. "Hold it," he called.

The only answer was the sound of the door closing.

Bill switched on lights ahead of him and went toward the sound — went through what was evidently a living room, through a small dining room, into a kitchen beyond. He took his revolver from its shoulder holster as he went.

A kitchen door led out into the rear court. Bill opened the door, and the court was empty. But now, again, he heard footsteps.

They were the steps of a man hurrying, but not quite running, and the man was hurrying on cement — along the driveway between the house and the one next to it, toward the street. Bill ran down a short flight of wooden stairs, and along the driveway.

He reached the sidewalk and, as far as he could see in either direction, it was empty. Bill swore, realizing what had happened. The man, on reaching the sidewalk, had merely run to the next driveway — but to right? or to left? — and then down it to another rear court. And then, for all Bill knew, had gone over a fence.

It would be possible to spend the rest of the night chasing this quarry up and down driveways, over fences. Probably, it would be a waste of the rest of the night. Bill put his revolver back in the holster and went into the house by the front door. On the chance, he turned out the lights and stood by the door and looked out of it through the glass panel.

A car came along the street, slowly, eased into the curb in front of Bill's Buick, hesitated there for a moment. A man came out from between houses, crossed the sidewalk and got into the car, which started up immediately.

There was a street light there, and Bill saw the man's face; he saw, and memorized the license number of the car — a not recent Ford sedan.

So, he thought, John Baker was a jump ahead. He seemed quite a man to jump ahead.

Bill turned from the door and regarded the telephone. It would be interesting to see what happened if he directed a pickup of the Ford sedan. After thought, he decided against it.

"Is a puzzlement," Pamela North said, quoting the king of Siam, without permission of the copyright owners. "There's too much of everything." She used fingers to note those things of which there was too much, one finger for each superfluity. "Mr. Monteath killing the first burglar," Pam North said. "Mr. Behren, with an 'H' being killed in New Guinea, but Mr. Barron with two 'R's' being at the party and being the other Mr. Behren. Mr. Frank finding Mr. Parsons's topcoat, but I don't believe for a minute there was blood on it."

"As Frank said," Jerry told her. "No blood."

"Only so everybody'd think there was," Pam said. "That's clear if anything is. And all this business about his mother!"

"I wasn't taken with Frank either," Jerry admitted. "Which isn't evidence, any more than the cats. About Baker, I mean."

Pam said she knew what he meant. She said it was unnecessary, as he should know, to dot every "T." She said that she still thought the cats were right, and where was she?

She was in front of a living room fire, which

was not needed, except that April is notoriously an uncertain month. She was in a housecoat. As she talked, she wriggled her feet out of slippers, wiggled her toes in the fire's warmth. Jerry, in polo shirt and slacks, sat with a long drink almost untouched beside him and regarded his wife's toes with relaxed pleasure. A fire, a lady of one's own, a drink — Jerry did not particularly want the drink; it remained a symbol of comfort.

"Well," Pam said, "where? If my toes bother you, I'll sit on them."

"Not in the least," Jerry said. "Very nice. At Mr. Frank, verging on Mr. Baker. There was also, as I recall it, something about dotting 'T's'."

"All right," Pam said, " 'I's,' then."

"Youse what?" Jerry asked her, with interest.

" 'I's' dotted," Pam said. "Please, Jerry. This is serious." She leaned forward, toward him. "Jerry, I'm worried."

She did not look it, Jerry told her. She looked —

"Now," Pam said. "All at once. Worried about Martha Evitts. It's all very well for us to sit here, with our own cats — where are they, by the way? I — "

Jerry pointed to a chair. In the seat of the chair there was a coil of cats. Teeney opened

243

blue eyes briefly, blinked, three times, and closed her eyes again.

" — and that poor thing, not knowing which way to turn."

She had known, Jerry pointed out. She had turned to John Baker; gone with John Baker. She was all right.

"Not if he isn't," Pam said. "*And,* he isn't. You didn't see him."

"Listen," Jerry said, fighting for the relaxed comfort, for the lazy warmth of the little fire. "Listen — you told Bill that Baker was here, that the girl went with him. A minute ago you were all right, wiggling your toes. Now — "

"We went off at so many angles," Pam said. "When Bill was here. I'd almost forgotten, because of all these other things — Mr. Monteath and Mr. Barron, however you spell it, and Frank and — "

"Yes," Jerry said. "Well, you told Bill. Bill will have somebody keep an eye on Martha. We can sit here and twiddle our toes and — how about a nightcap?"

"No," Pam said, and her tone was abstracted. "And I don't think it's good for you to drink after dinner. Remember how you felt this morning."

"I feel fine now," Jerry said, "and — " But he stopped, because he was not being listened to. Pam stood up suddenly. As if girding herself, she belted the housecoat more closely about her, which was becoming.

"I've got to be sure she's all right," Pam said. "She came here for help and I — I didn't do anything. And — "

It was gone, Jerry realized. The fire no longer glowed softly, but crackled. Small toes no longer twinkled idly; they were about to be walked on.

"Mercurial," Jerry said, half to himself.

"What?"

"Never mind," he said.

"Bill may have forgotten too," Pam said. "I'm going to call her up."

It was contagious. This is ridiculous, Jerry told himself. At one moment we are — well, purring in front of a fire. At the next, with nothing changed — nothing we know of changed — things are urgent again. We arch our backs and bush our tails and — *damn it, maybe Pam is right about Baker. Maybe she didn't make it important enough to Bill.*

Pam had the Manhattan telephone book. It was on the floor and she was kneeling in front of it, turning pages.

"R, S, T, U, V," Pam North said. "E V — Evans — Evers — Evinson — Ewans — I've gone too far — Evis — *Evitts*. Martha Evitts."

She pivoted to sit on the floor, slim legs escaping the housecoat, extending in front of her. She spun the dial. She waited, hearing a telephone ring. It rang, and rang again and yet again.

"Jerry!" Pam said. "She's not — "

"Sorry," a female voice said — a young female voice said — "I was in the tub, of course. Hello?"

"Martha?" Pam said. "Miss Evitts?"

"Afraid she's not here," the voice said. "I live here with her — this is Paula." She waited a moment. "Paula Thompson," she said. "I'm sorry, Martha just left this minute."

"She's all right?"

"Why — sure. Why wouldn't she be? Oh — you mean because this man she worked for got killed?"

"Partly," Pam said. "This is Mrs. Gerald North. I saw Miss Evitts this afternoon and — "

"He was just a man she worked for," Paula said. "For goodness' sake, Mrs. — North, was it?"

"Yes," Pam said.

"I'm sorry," Paula said. "Look, I'm dripping all over the rug. I'll tell Martha you called, if I'm here when she gets back. I've got sort of a late date and — "

"Wait," Pam said. "Please wait. She was

in this evening?"

"For a while. Then this man called her."

"Mr. Baker?"

Paula Thompson sneezed.

"If I catch another cold," she said, direfully. "Maybe. But this was business. Now, before I catch — "

"Please," Pam said. "I know it's dreadful. But — what kind of business?"

"My teeth are starting to chatter," Paula said. "This place she works. All I know is, this man called her up. She talked to him. She said, 'Well, it ought to be. I put it there.' And then, 'All right. I suppose I'll have to.' Then she hung up and said she had to go down to the place she works and — a-chew!"

"The man who called her," Pam said. "I'm terribly sorry, Miss Thompson. It can be important. Didn't she say who it was?"

"Just somebody from the office," Paula said. "She didn't say who. Oh damn it! There's my date at the door and here I am — I've simply got to — "

"Goodbye," Pam said. "I — I hope you don't really catch cold."

She put the receiver back. She looked at it.

"She's gone to that — place," Pam said. "The Novelty something. Where she works. And — somebody called and told her to go there. I'm sure it was Mr. Baker. And — "

Pam had pivoted again. She was on her knees again, flipping pages of the telephone book. "H-I-J-K-L-M," Pam said. "I wish I didn't always have to go through the whole alphabet to get N. J-K-L-M-N-O — Novelty — Novelty what?"

"Emporium," Jerry said.

"Emporium," Pam said, and whirled again, and dialed again. And again a telephone rang repeatedly. But this time, although Pam gave it time enough and more, the telephone was not answered.

For the third number she called, at twenty minutes past nine that Thursday evening, Pam did not need to refer to the directory, and the telephone was answered promptly. But neither Captain Weigand nor Sergeant Mullins was in the office. They would be told that she had called.

"*Jerry,*" Pam said. "Nobody knows but us. Nobody who would understand. Come *on,* Jerry!"

Pam was on her feet, she went down the hall toward the bedroom, and the housecoat billowed behind her as she loosened it; it was slipping from her shoulders as she went through the door.

"Oh God!" Jerry North said, and went for a jacket. It was not, he decided, an occasion which was going to call for a necktie. He wondered, uneasily, what it would call for.

Bill Weigand is not a man to lose himself twice in the same terrain. He drove the long way out of Brooklyn without hesitation, as one familiar with the borough's ramifications. Once you got the hang of things —

As he drove, not much hurrying, stopping obediently for lights, Bill hoped he had the hang of things. The case had its ramifications, like the borough. But once you got the hang of them — once you knew enough to guess the shape — it all became reasonable enough. There might be side issues; certainly there were areas unexplored. And what might come next could only be guessed at. It would come within certain boundaries, the boundaries which outlined the shape of murder — and that other shape which concerned Saul Bessing.

It had been difficult to fit together a topcoat, which might or might not have blood on it, and a dummy "defenestrated" — although not precisely that; apparently there had been no ejection through a window — and fingerprints in a safe. Where Maine fitted in had not been immediately apparent, and John Baker's part had been only something to guess at. But now, Bill decided — going onto the approach of the Manhattan Bridge — it was simple enough.

It was not as simple, unfortunately for him, as one person had thought it would be. Yet it was hard to see what, having once made up his mind as to what was most expedient, the person in question could have done, even had he known of the ramifications. (One had to postulate that, still only to be guessed at, there was a specific motive of great importance. The motive, presumably, still prevailed.)

Bill hoped that Mr. Bertram Dewsnap knew what he was about — what he was about when he left his house in Brooklyn and took off in whatever direction, for whatever purpose, he had found impelling. Bill had searched the house, after he had watched John Baker starting on his ride, and had found what he expected to find — nothing and nobody. Nobody on the first floor, nobody on the second or third. (And not much furniture on the upper floors, either. Mr. Dewsnap was not really settled in. It had probably not seemed worth the trouble, since in his trade one is very apt to be here today and gone tomorrow.) There had been nothing in the basement except an oil burner and two metal cans, one half full of the debris of (light) housekeeping; the other empty. In a closet in the basement, which Bill had opened with some interest, there had been nothing. A body would have fitted into it neatly enough; none did.

Bill had called his office, got Mullins. He heard the essentials of Mullins's interview with Mrs. Wilmot and Clyde Parsons. "He could of got in and killed Wilmot," Mullins pointed out. "But if Mrs. Wilmot is telling the truth, there wouldn't have been much time."

"Right," Bill said. "We'll talk to them tomorrow — if we need to by then. And — "

He had been asked to hold it for a moment. Mullins had conferred with someone else, said, "Hm-m" to someone else, and returned. "Mrs. Wilmot and Parsons are off some place," he said. "The man who was staked out went along. Hasn't called in, yet."

Bill had thought of that for a moment. Then he had told Sergeant Mullins what he wanted done.

So now there was no real reason for Bill to hurry. Yet, as he came down into Manhattan, and familiar streets, he began to push the Buick a little. He still did not use his siren, but he did not lag.

Sylvester Frank had expected to have a night off, even if in jail. That, as he had understood it, had been the program. It appeared that the program had been changed. Released

251

in the custody of his attorney — whom he had never seen before; not before suspected the existence of — Frank had been told where to go. He was now on his way there, presumably for further instructions. He had to assume, he supposed, that there had been a slip-up. Or, of course, that he had been picked for something else.

Well, he couldn't say "no." He realized that. Anything in reason — like telling certain things and getting himself arrested — had got to be done. The trouble was, one could never tell what would be considered in reason. He hoped knives wouldn't come into it again. All day he had been remembering; had been sharing, although without knowing it, Lady Macbeth's surprise at the amount of blood one man has in him.

Well, once you got yourself into things like this, you followed instructions and hoped for the best.

Albert Barron, as he preferred nowadays to think of himself, sat in one end of a subway car, and read a newspaper, which he held well in front of his face. Each time the train stopped, Mr. Barron refolded his newspaper and, in the process, looked out from behind it. The girl remained at the other end of the car, and remained alone.

The whole procedure struck him as rather absurd. The girl had no reason to suspect anything amiss; it would have been simpler not to complicate matters more than they already were complicated.

If things went much further, Mr. Barron told himself, looking with a marked lack of interest at stock market quotations, he was getting out. There were other ways of making a living and, on the whole, safer ones. They had never laid hands on him in the old days.

For a while longer he would play along, obey instructions, and see. But only for a time, and as long as the instructions were reasonable and didn't require that he further risk his neck. That, he had risked enough already.

The sergeant who had gone to the penthouse at about two-thirty that morning and conversed, through a closed door, with a man who was soon to be dead — he was, Weigand had been able to remember, named after some animal. It took Mullins time to identify the sergeant; there had been some effort to persuade him to accept a Sergeant Katz, but Katz had been nowhere near the penthouse. Mullins tried again.

"Oh, you mean Fox," the precinct lieutenant said. "Why didn't you say so, man? He's out in a prowl. Weigand wants him particularly?"

"Yes," Mullins said, "that's what he says, lieutenant."

"Why? Fox never saw this dead man of yours."

"I'm afraid I don't know," Mullins said. "The captain didn't say. Just said — get hold of this sergeant and take him along with you."

"O.K.," the lieutenant said. "Anything to oblige Homicide. Where you want him to meet you?"

Mullins told him.

Mr. Bertram Dewsnap let himself into the front door of the Novelty Emporium. He left the door unlocked behind him for the rest to follow. The ground floor showroom was large, and shadowy. Halfway down its length, on the mezzanine above it, a single light bulb burned behind the sliding glass window of Mr. Dewsnap's own office — burned like a small, watchful eye, on duty when other eyes were closed. The light from this bulb created the shadows in the broad area below — shadows of costumes on clothing dummies and on racks; shadows of masks hanging on hooks above showcases. The shadows further distorted the already distorted masks and to some of them seemed to impart a kind of fantastic life. One of them, a Punch with a great, curved nose, seemed to follow with blank eyes Mr. Dewsnap's progress through the showroom to the narrow stairs which led up to his office. But Mr. Dewsnap paid no attention to this, being habituated to the oddities of the Novelty Emporium.

Mr. Dewsnap had several things to do and several people to see. Then — and this thought pleased him as he sat down at his desk to wait — things would be wound up. They would be wound up not too soon but not, he was certain, too late, either. The last was what mattered, of course — mattered personally. Things had been getting tighter for some time, and he had known men — even men in the business — who go nervous when things tightened. Sometimes, to put it simply, they stampeded. A stampede is dangerous, being unplanned and beyond control. If you worked things out, and used your head — and your experience — you could slip through the vise jaws just before the pinch came. Mr. Dewsnap had done it often enough before. He had the skill which comes from experience.

The lack of that experience, Mr. Dewsnap could only assume, was what had been Wilmot's undoing. Wilmot — although that last trick of his had been ingenious in conception — had been really an amateur, with an amateur's inclination to go at things in a heavy-handed fashion. If your hands were too heavy, you left no alternative — no safe alternative — to those upon whom you applied pressure. This could be dangerous, as Wilmot had discovered. On the whole, Wilmot was no great loss; his death had, indeed, turned out to have a certain indirect advantage. That had been apparent since the telephone call which had brought Mr. Dewsnap out of his house in Brooklyn.

Not, of course, that Mr. Dewsnap had planned to remain there much longer in any case. The whole thing was played out, and the Brooklyn house with the rest. That had been probable since Wilmot's death; it had been certain since Mr. Dewsnap, who could see a good deal through the window of his office, who could see the whole length of the showroom and into the street beyond the glass front doors, had observed Mr. Baker loitering. "Loitering with intent," as the British put it. The intent had been obvious. It had made Mr. Baker obvious, but Mr. Dewsnap had already been fairly certain about Mr. Baker. Not that Mr. Baker hadn't done a reasonably professional job. Mr. Dewsnap, talking from experience, would give him that. Mr. Dewsnap now bore Mr. Baker's competence in mind — and had arranged accordingly.

By midnight, Mr. Dewsnap decided, he would be out of it. They would all be out of it. It was too bad about the money, but there was nothing to be done about it, and it was not really important. Within a day or two, there would be more money — plenty more money. It would have been neater to have picked up everything in Mr. Wilmot's safe — money and whatever else was there — but the opportunity had not arisen.

Mr. Dewsnap waited at his desk. In due course Mr. Dewsnap heard feet on the wooden stairs to the mezzanine.

XI

Thursday, 10:22 P.M. *to* 11:12 P.M.

Martha Evitts hesitated at the door. She looked through a glass panel into the shadowy interior of the Emporium. It was impossible that she had misunderstood, had not been told to come tonight, to come at once; had not been told, clearly, that she was needed to help get "things straightened out."

She had not wanted to come, had thought of pretending illness, of saying that the shock of her experience that morning was still too great. And she had promised John to stay in the apartment until he came for her. But the word "ought" had come into it; "you ought to come if you possibly can." The word "ought," representing an obligation, was a compelling word. And it was true — she supposed it was true — that Mr. Wilmot's sudden death had left things disorderly in the business of which he had been, so personally, the head. "At sixes and sevens," she had been told, and told again she was needed.

She had got a picture in her mind, from that. All the others who worked at the Emporium were there, trying to get things straightened out. Mr. Dewsnap, of course, and Mr. Barron. But others of the office staff, too, and the floor workers — the salesmen, the stock clerks, the section heads. She had pictured bustle, with all lights on, with everyone responding to emergency. And it was reasonable that she, as Mr. Wilmot's secretary — as the person in the office most likely to know what had been in his mind — would be, as much as anyone except Mr. Dewsnap himself, needed to get things organized.

But now there was no sign of people responding to emergency. So far as she could tell, from outside, looking in, the Emporium was deserted. Only the single night light burned dimly behind the sliding window of Mr. Dewsnap's mezzanine office. In the showroom there were only shadows.

After a moment, an obvious explanation occurred to Martha. She was merely the first to arrive. She opened her handbag and searched in it for her key to the front door. She found the little chain of keys — keys of her own; keys which were part of her job, so that she could open the front door and the side door, the "alley door," of the Emporium, and the door of Mr. Wilmot's penthouse. She must remember to give that one to somebody; she decided that, when everything was "straightened out," she would give the other business keys to somebody, too. There would be other jobs.

But now she still had a job, and she was the first to respond to the summons. That was all. Mr. Dewsnap himself, and probably Mr. Barron, would be in the large office Mr. Wilmot had used behind the mezzanine, where lights would be burning that she could not see from the front door.

She opened the door and went into the shadows. The light switch for the showroom was on the wall near the stairs to the mezzanine; when she reached it she would see that there was light. She went down the center aisle, and grotesque faces seemed to nod as she passed. It was easy to imagine that hanging costumes — costumes for witches, for the associates of witches and for the master of all witches — swayed toward her, reached out toward her their armless sleeves.

Martha Evitts had not been there before at night, in the shadows. She told herself that all these were commonplace by light — that they were papier mâché masks and dusty, empty garments. But she hurried toward the light.

She hurried so that she almost did not see, in time, what lay on the floor, in the center of the aisle, precisely below the window of Mr. Dewsnap's mezzanine office. It was only a darker shadow, but she stopped in time. It was a costume, thrown down on the tiled floor, crumpled there in a heap. It had to be that — it could not be —

Knowing what it was, but refusing to know, Martha stood and looked down. And then, from blood spreading — *again blood spreading* — from the shattered head Martha shrank back. Sickness rose in her, into her throat. And now darkness seemed to swirl around her in a cloud, with herself in a circle of light, but with the circle shrinking.

She looked away from the body on the floor — from the blood, and not only blood, around the head. She looked up at the mezzanine and saw the sliding window open; looked through it and saw a man at Mr. Dewsnap's desk. The dim light was on his face.

It was not Mr. Dewsnap's face. Mr. Dewsnap's face was hidden. It was against the tile of the floor, with blood spreading around it.

The swirl of blackness encroached on the little circle of light. And in the circle now there was only a face — not her own face, not the face crushed on the tile. *John Baker's face.* John's face intent in the dim light as he bent over the desk of a dead man, peered into a drawer of the dead man's desk.

John, she thought, and thought she said,

but she made no sound. *John — John — John —*

The circle of light in which she lived, in which consciousness lived, was very small. It was large as a quarter, as a dime, as the head of —

She turned from the body, fighting sickness, fighting the darkness. She clutched at a counter and dislodged something, and a snake fell from the counter and seemed to writhe toward the body. Martha did not know of this, did not hear the tiny sound.

John Baker heard it, and looked out. But as he looked, Martha Evitts — putting her head down against faintness, fighting the blackness — slumped to the floor beside the counter, and so slumped into the dark.

Baker looked for a moment, went back to his scrutiny of the contents of the desk drawer.

He did not look up again at the small sounds Martha Evitts made as, still fearing to stand erect, knowing that if she stood the light circle — a little larger now — would shrink again, and to nothingness, she went on her knees, in the shadow of counters, toward the door of the Emporium.

I've got to get away, her mind said. *I've got to get away. He mustn't see me, mustn't see me, mustn't see me. He'll hurt me if he finds me.*

John will hurt me. John. John . . .

She could not stop the meaningless words. They rattled in her mind.

She was near the door, but still in shadow, when the turmoil began to recede a little, when the darkness no longer seemed to sweep in spirals so closely around her.

She saw, then, that that way was blocked. Inside the door, his back to her, a man was standing. He wore a long coat. He, too, seemed just to have come out of the shadows, but of that she could not be sure. He stood only a moment, silhouetted against the light which came from the street through the glass panels. There was nothing threatening about him as he stood there. But he was a threat.

She had to get away — far away, away alone. She had to reach, first of all, a quiet place, where the rattling in her mind might stop. She fled the horror behind her — the crushed head on the floor, the blood around it, the grayness mingled with the blood. She fled danger. But she could not — not now, not while her mind was ungovernable — flee to safety, because, with safety found, she would have to tell what she had seen — all she had seen. And that would mean that John —

Somebody else would find out; somebody else would tell. But not she — *not she*. She would save that — that little thing, that pitiably little thing. She wouldn't have been the one.

Still crouching, she went between counters, to another aisle. Still crouching, still in the shadows, she went down that aisle toward the rear of the store. Beyond the mezzanine, where darkness would be almost complete, she would stand up again. There she would cross the store, find the alley exit. She would go very slowly, very carefully, and she would reach the door, and she would go out into the night, and then she would be alone. . . .

The man who had been by the door drew back, first into the shadows, then, very cautiously, behind a rack of costumes. From there, peering between a gaudy scarlet cape and a black sheath painted with a skeleton's bones — both very limp without occupants — he watched another man try the door, find it unlocked, open it slowly. The first man moved further into the costume racks, and waited.

The second man came into the showroom and stopped, and looked around. He stood irresolutely for a moment, and then started up the central aisle.

Now was the time, the man behind the costume racks decided, and began to move. As he moved the skeleton moved, too, swaying in the shadows, its bones white against black. The man paused to check its revealing motion, and then stepped back again. It was too late, now. Somebody else was outside the door — no, two people were outside the door.

The man behind the skeleton swore soundlessly. These two wouldn't have come alone, or be alone long if they had. He began to move, very cautiously, behind the racks, toward the rear of the store. . . .

"You saw him," Pamela North said. "He just opened the door and walked in. Mr. Baker."

She didn't, Jerry said, know it was Mr. Baker. It was just a man, admittedly of about the right size, although in dim light it was difficult to tell about size. Furthermore, if Mr. Baker, he worked at the Emporium, which made it different. For them to go into an obviously closed store, even if someone had neglected to lock the door, would be —

But by that time, Pam North had opened the door, and was going through it. Inside, however, she paused, she looked around.

"Spooky," she said. "Full of — things." She looked around, she shrank back a little against Jerry. *"Look!"* she said, and the word was whispered. "That — *thing* — it's moving." She shrank more closely. "It's a skeleton," she said, and pointed.

Jerry could just make it out. It was not, so far as he could see, moving. He said so;

he told her to look again. She did.

"Well," Pam said, "I thought it was. This is an awful place."

"This," Gerald North said, "is a perfectly ordinary store where they happen to sell costumes, and masks, and — "

"Snakes and spiders," Pam said. "I know. It doesn't help particularly."

"Then," Jerry said, "let's get out of it. We haven't any business here. If you still think that Miss Evitts is in some sort of danger, we can — "

"Jerry," Pam said. "We just stand here! And we don't know what he's doing to Martha. We — "

She started up the central aisle, through the shadows. Jerry went after her.

It did not take them long.

Pam came on it first, and too closely on it. She stopped with the toes of shoes in blood, and as she shrank back, made a small, sick, wordless sound, her shoes left dabs of blood on tiles.

Jerry crouched by the body, peered at it, and thought that what he did was senseless. The smallish man in the gray suit — but the suit was no longer entirely gray — was as beyond help as — as Humpty Dumpty, Jerry thought, as Humpty Dumpty fallen from the wall, as — Damn this place, Jerry thought, and stood up.

"Never saw him before," he said. "From what Bill told us, a man named Dewsnap. Managed the place for Wilmot — *Pam!*"

Pam did not appear to be listening. She was looking up at the mezzanine, at an empty office dimly lighted by a single bulb in the ceiling, at an open sliding window. She did not appear to hear Jerry, but she had heard.

"Mr. Dewsnap," she said. "Yes. Somebody dropped him, Jerry. Dropped him — *upside down!*"

Jerry looked up, looked down again at what was broken on the floor. He nodded slowly. It seemed very likely that somebody had dropped Mr. Dewsnap; had held him head down out of the mezzanine window, had dropped him head-first to the tile floor a dozen feet below.

"There's a telephone up there," Pam said. "I'll — "

"Wait," Jerry said.

"Not here," Pam said. "Not with — " She broke off. "There must be stairs," she said. "There'd have to be, wouldn't there? You stay. I'll — "

She was gone, then. She went around the body, close to a counter on her right, her head averted. Her body seemed queerly rigid in the shadows.

Jerry hesitated. She was right. It was no place to stay. He was himself fighting nausea; he could watch Pam in the office above; he could — By that time it was decided for him. Pam had disappeared around the end of the counter.

But she couldn't wander alone in the darkness, Jerry thought, and moved, and at the same time heard a sound which seemed to come from behind the counter along which Pam had walked. He moved quickly to the counter, and leaned over it. He saw a darker shadow there, but not in time. There was a great noise, but it was inside the skull of Gerald North. Gerald North staggered back from the counter, reeled halfway across the aisle, grabbed the counter on the other side just as blackness engulfed him. He tried to fight it off, tried to stand up, and lost the fight. . . .

Pam found the stairs. She went up them, came to a door and opened it and was in the office. She could have looked down from the open window, and she would have seen more than she expected. But she had seen enough. She kept her back to the window; she faced a closed door in the wall opposite the window. She reached for the telephone on the desk, and the door by which she had entered opened.

"Jerry," Pam said, "I'm so glad you — "
And then she cried, loudly, *"Jerry! Jerry!"*
because it was not Jerry at the door, coming
into the office.

Mr. Punch came through the door; Punch
with a great hooked nose; Punch red-faced
and leering. But it was not the dwarfed, round
Punch. The head of Punch was atop a tall
figure in a black robe, a robe on which stars
were scattered. The figure raised an arm and
pointed at her.

"Don't use that," the towering Punch said,
in a strange, muffled voice — a slurred voice;
an unrecognizable voice. "Jush — "

Punch advanced and Pam cried, once more,
"Jerry!" and then jumped for the door in the
wall opposite the window.

"I'm not — " Punch said in the same muffled, jumbled voice, and took another step.
But Pam had reached the door, thrown herself
against it as she turned the knob, and was
in a corridor beyond. The door remained open
behind her, and there was faint light from the
office bulb. Then the light was almost blotted
out by a moving shadow, and on the wall
ahead, and to her left, there was momentarily
the wavering outline of Punch's great, mis-
shapen nose, grown in the shadow infinitely
monstrous.

Pam North ran down a corridor between

doors. Ahead was only darkness. She ran in shadow; she held out a hand on either side to ward away the walls. It seemed that the corridor would never end, and that the shadow pursued.

The corridor ended. Just before she hurtled down a steep flight of wooden stairs, Pam caught herself by the railings on either side. For a moment she hung over the steps, her weight wrenching at her handholds. But then she regained her balance. She went down the stairs, dropped down them, sustained by the railings.

Far beyond her, tall windows let in a little light. There was enough light to see that she was in another spreading, shadowy room, with counters like the room in the front of the building, again with racks along the walls and things dangling from them, like men and women hanging.

The mezzanine from which she had come was a wide bridge across an enormous room. Corridors ran under it. If she could run back through one of the corridors, she could get to where Jerry was.

She turned to her left, and moved again between counters. On one of the counters, the one on her right, she could just make out the dull gleam of — she checked herself for an instant, and looked unbelievingly. Arranged neatly on the wooden top of a counter were a dozen automatic pistols. Pam North seized the nearest and went on.

She came to a corridor which, since it again ran to her left, must go under the mezzanine bridge. It was almost completely dark in the corridor. Pam held the pistol tightly, a little in front of her, and plunged into the darkness.

Almost instantly, she walked into something, and the something was soft and yielding — and human. For a moment, Pam was locked with the other as in an embrace, and then each pushed against the other and Martha Evitts said:

"*John. No!*" And then, "*You're not John!*" Martha spoke softly, her voice reedy.

"Sh-h!" Pam said, and whispered. "It's Pam North. *Punch is chasing me.*"

She reached out and held Martha's arm.

"I've got a gun," Pam said. "We'll — "

"Let me go," Martha said. "Can't you understand? Let me go. John isn't here. He didn't — "

She pushed at Pam, trying to get past her.

"Wait," Pam said. "I don't know whether John Baker's here. He could — somebody's dressed as Punch. And somebody killed Mr. Dewsnap. Somebody dropped — "

"You've got to let me go!" Martha said, and pushed and Pam took a step back in the darkness and would have fallen but someone caught her.

"What the devil?" a man's voice said, harshly, and a thin, questing ray of light shot out and fell on Pam North's face, moved to Martha's face.

"John," Martha said. "Don't — don't — "

The man had a revolver in his hand. He was not pointing it, but it was ready. The pencil of light had not found the automatic in Pam North's hand. She raised it, pointed it in the general direction of the light.

"Let us go or — " Pam said and then, convulsive, with the automatic pointing at the man, she pressed a trigger.

A balloon — a quite large, vari-colored balloon — spread itself from the muzzle of the automatic. It squeezed itself out and spread and spread, and then it floated prettily from a cord in a narrow shaft of light, at the end of the automatic. Pam stared at the balloon without belief.

Then she turned and tried to run, but Martha Evitts blocked her progress in one direction and the man with the light in the other.

Pam used the automatic as a club, the balloon wavering grotesquely, and swung it at the hand which held the light. Martha cried, *"Don't! It's John!"* and the butt of the automatic hit the metal of the flashlight with a sharp sound and the light went out and down and clattered on the floor.

"Of all the — " the man said, and grabbed at the automatic and the balloon gave a loud "pop!" in the darkness. Pam leaped to the side, holding Martha's hand, dragging at her. For an instant, Martha Evitts resisted; then she came. A hand caught at Pam, held briefly to the fabric of her blouse, and the blouse gave.

"You little idiots," the man said. "Wait. Don't you — "

They heard him. They did not stop. They ran out of the corridor into the rear showroom. Silhouetted against one of the distant windows, Punch towered. At the sound of their running, Punch turned toward them.

"I know it's John," Martha said. "I — "

"With Punch's head," Pam said, in a whisper. "Under here."

Jerry came out of the blackness and pulled himself up, holding to the counter. He was on his feet, but the room wavered around him. He had to get to Pam.

Holding to the counter, while the room still wavered, he looked up at the mezzanine window. He could see all of the little office and it was empty. No — he could not see it all.

He could not see the floor of the office. Pam was not standing there, not at the telephone on the desk. She might be —

His legs were lead; his whole body seemed numb. There was a man somewhere who was quick and merciless, who — He heard a sound, but as he stood it was behind him. He turned, slowly, painfully, and between him and the entrance door there was a man, coming toward him.

Jerry forced himself to stand unsupported in the aisle; forced himself to walk — although in reality he staggered — toward the man, whose face was a blur in the light. The man stopped and stared at him.

"Slug me, will you," Jerry said, and swung at the man while he was still some feet from him. Jerry swayed and the man caught hold of him, and held him.

"And what," Sergeant Mullins said, "is the matter with you, Mr. North?"

"Teach you to — " Jerry said, and struggled for a moment and his head cleared. "Got slugged," Jerry said, in his own voice. "Pam went to — " He remembered it all, now, more clearly. "Up there," he said, and pointed.

They looked up at the window of the mezzanine office. A tall figure in black stood there. It wore the head of Punch, the immortal. It looked down at them through Punch's eyes.

Then it turned, and seemed to stalk toward the rear of the room.

"What goes on here?" Mullins said, in a voice that filled the spreading room. "In the name of all the saints — *what goes on here?!*"

Martha Evitts was saying, "No, you don't understand. The other man — not — not the man with the mask" and Pam said, "Listen. Listen!"

And then Pam North stuck her head out from under the counter where she had pulled Martha Evitts, pushing aside the black stuff which had curtained them, and spoke. Pam North yelled.

"Mullins!" Pam cried. "Sergeant *Mullins! Watch out for Mr. Punch!*" She paused, gathered breath. "Jerry!" She yelled. "Jer-*ree*. I'm *here!*"

It was perhaps the least illuminating remark Pamela North had ever made. But she made it loudly.

And then, all over the considerable area of the Novelty Emporium, lights went on.

Light changed everything. All that had been shadow and strange was harshly obvious and, if still strange, so without eeriness. But there was more than that — noise gave place to silence, violent action to cautious movement. And everything — to Pam, standing in an aisle with Martha Evitts beside her — happened at once.

Jerry ran, and staggered as he ran, down a passage under the mezzanine bridge, and another man ran after him, apparently in pursuit. A smallish man dodged back and forth around a table which was piled with dolls, and two men dodged this way and that with him, in a kind of dance. He broke and ran and one caught him roughly; Jerry was beside Pam and had his arms around her — and to some degree around Martha Evitts, also — and the man who had pursued Jerry was Sergeant Mullins, who ran on past the three of them toward several men who seemed just to have entered the room — but from a doorway at the rear, not under the mezzanine.

Then, through another passage under the mezzanine, a uniformed patrolman came running. Just as he reached the second room, he stopped and turned. In an instant he was grappling with still another man. They swayed for a moment, clinching, and then the man not in uniform freed himself. He turned a little as he did so, and there was light on his face and he was John Baker.

Martha Evitts screamed, and then cried: *"No. John! Don't!"* but John Baker, moving so quickly that the movement could hardly be seen, struck the policeman on the side of the jaw and the policeman staggered, revolved slowly and collapsed. Mullins veered in an aisle toward Baker and had his revolver ready and a voice came sharply from among the men who had entered by the rear door. "Hold it, sergeant," the voice said, commanding, and Mullins half turned, blank surprise on his face. "Right," Bill Weigand said. "Hold it." Weigand ran toward Baker and Mullins and brushed a table as he ran. Toads of many sizes spewed from the table spreading, bouncing, on the floor.

"Where is he?" Weigand called, as he ran, and Baker said, "Somewhere around" and then, "Where's Saul?"

"Front," Bill said.

Then Baker, who was looking beyond Weigand, said loudly, "Stop him, damn it!" and a man in civilian clothes pounced like a big cat on the smallish man, who had dodged so agilely and had somehow, momentarily, dodged free.

One of the men who had come in with Bill Weigand said, "*Look, for God's sake!*" and pointed toward a far corner of the room — the corner nearest the rear windows, most distant from all of them.

There was a spiral iron staircase there. A grotesque figure in black, the black spangled with stars, was going up the staircase. As the man who had seen him first shouted again and pointed, the spiral brought the figure around again and it looked down at them from the face of Mr. Punch. As the figure paused for an instant his grotesque shadow hesitated on the wall beyond.

Then the figure went on up the stairs.

"The door's locked," Martha Evitts said, tensely, beside Pam. "It's always locked!"

The figure had reached the top of the spiral stairs, and the door there. The black robe hid movement, but it was clear Punch tried the door — clear, as he turned, that the door had stopped him.

Men were running toward the staircase then — there were half a dozen men running down aisles, around tables. Baker bent quickly over the policeman on the floor, and did something, and then ran with the others toward Mr. Punch.

Mr. Punch stood at the top of the stairs and looked down at them all.

"They were all rats," Mr. Punch said, rather loudly, but in the same muffled, slurred voice Pam had heard before.

"Hey," one of the men who looked up said, and said it in a tone of utter surprise. "That's the man who — that man's *dead*."

"It is, Fox," Bill Weigand said. "But he isn't — *don't do that!*"

"Why?" Mr. Punch asked.

He had something in his hand; the light glittered on it — on the blade of a knife.

Mr. Punch held the knife, with its long blade pointed inward toward himself, and held it with both hands. He held it so for an instant, looking down at it, and then plunged the knife toward his own chest — plunged it until hands met chest, the hilt of the knife between them.

He held it so, for a second, and then slowly moved his hands away and looked down at them. Only the hilt was between the hands. The blade had broken —

Mr. Punch laughed, then — a high, strange laugh. He opened the clasped hands and the hilt of the knife fell from them, and began to clatter down the stairs. As it bounced, the blade shot out from the hilt and the thing was a knife again — as much of a knife as it had ever been.

"You may as well come down, Monteath," Bill Weigand said, mildly.

"Yes," Arthur Monteath said, from behind the grotesque mask of Mr. Punch. "You do seem to have won the last trick, don't you?"

Arthur Monteath came down the circular stair. In spite of the steepness of the stairs, the impediment of the long, starred robe, his descent was not without dignity.

Friday, 5:45 P.M. *to* 7:10 P.M.

Dorian Weigand sat in a deep chair, her right foot tucked under her left leg. A Siamese cat lay on her lap. A drawing pad rested on the cat, and Dorian made a picture on the pad — a picture of a towering astrologer with the head of Mr. Punch, standing at the top of a spiral staircase. The down-hooking nose of Mr. Punch all but met the chin which spiked up beneath it. Mr. Punch was in his most malevolent mood, and he cast a grotesque shadow on the wall.

"Was that the way it looked?" Dorian asked and Pam North, who stood above her, carrying a plate of olives and sliced raw carrots, said, "Um-m. Yes. Only worse, if anything. You don't show the knife. But — that's pretty much the way it looked. Olive?"

"It seems," Dorian said, "a little extreme, somehow. I guess not right now." The last appertained to the olive.

"Well," Pam said, "Mr. Monteath seems to be an extreme man. Dropping the dummy off the roof. To say nothing of poor Mr. Dewsnap on his head. To say nothing of Mr.

Wilmot, to begin with."

She gestured with the olive-carrot plate at Jerry North, who shuddered; at Bill Weigand, who merely shook his head. Pam took an olive. She looked at the carrots and said that what they needed was a rabbit. She returned to her own chair and sipped from the glass beside it.

"To be perfectly honest," Pam said, "I was surprised. But you weren't. That's why Sergeant Fox was there. To identify the voice. But you knew already."

This was to Bill Weigand, who sat in another chair, with another cat. The cat was Martini, and this was remarkable. Martini was more apt to nibble people (other than the Norths) than to sit on them.

"I told you you can always go by cats," Pam said to Jerry.

"You did indeed," Jerry said. "And you couldn't, as it turned out. Because, if you could have, Punch would have been Mr. Baker. And Mr. Baker is — what, Bill? FBI?"

"Near enough" Bill said, and did not amplify. They waited. "His name isn't Baker," Bill said. "He's older than he looks."

"Martha will like that," Pam said. "Of course, it will be confusing not knowing what her name is."

They all looked at her. Jerry blinked.

"They'd been after Mr. Wilmot for some time, then," Pam said. "Or was it more Mr. Dewsnap?"

Bill shrugged. He had not been informed; it was unlikely that he would be. At a guess — Dewsnap had headed it, had been the professional.

"A spy ring," Pam said. "Right here in this apartment house. Atom bombs and everything."

Bill said he gathered atom bombs, as such, had already been pretty well taken care of. There were other things — a good many other things. He hadn't been told what; wouldn't be told what. But — if she cared for the term — a spy ring.

"I like it very much," Pam said. "And Mr. Wilmot was sending plans of things disguised as plans for other things — I mean magic cabinets and what not — to — to whom?"

"I don't know," Bill said. "To anyone who would buy, I imagine. That was all the other side of it, Pam. Not our side. Of course, the two things dovetailed."

"Suppose," Dorian said, "somebody begins at the beginning? I came in at the end. This — " She gestured with the drawing pad. The cat on her lap stood up, arched back, revolved twice and sat down again. "Please, Sherry," Dorian said. "You don't need your spikes. I won't let you fall off. Well?"

Bill finished his drink. He looked at his empty glass. Jerry went for the shaker, mixed again, filled glasses.

"Now," Pam North said.

"It began with blackmail," Bill said. "Monteath admits that. Blackmail of his wife. He doesn't say what she had done — or what it could have been made to appear she had done. He says, 'I killed a man to keep a secret. Why should I tell it now?' Behren knows, of course. But Behren isn't in our hands. In any case, it doesn't matter too much. And — I probably wouldn't tell if I knew. The woman's dead. She's been dead a long time. She didn't want to live. In effect, she killed herself. When I found that out, there was a pattern."

"You knew more than we did," Pam said, with a somewhat defrauded air.

Bill admitted that. He said, mildly, that that, among other things, was what policemen were for.

"I wish," Dorian said, "that people would quit interrupting people."

Bill grinned at her. He said, "Right." He said it was this way.

Years before, in Maine, Arthur Monteath had killed a man he said was an unknown intruder who had tried to force his way into a seaside cottage. The local police accepted this. It was not true. The man Monteath had killed was one of two not very skillful blackmailers — apprentice blackmailers. The other had been a red-haired young man named Alexander Behren. Monteath admitted, now — now that he was admitting almost everything — that the man he killed, Parks, and Behren had come to the cottage by arrangement, to collect. But by the time they came, Monteath had decided not to pay, but to kill. His wife's heart attack which he blamed on the strain she had been under — "I don't know how justly," Bill said. "But it was what he thought" — had made him ready to kill. He had planned to kill both men. Behren had escaped.

Behren had not tried again, partly — one could guess — because he decided Monteath was too dangerous; partly because, with Mrs. Monteath dead, he had no safe victim. He could not tell what he knew about Parks's death without revealing what had taken him and Parks to the cottage. Shortly after, Behren had been inducted into the army. The whole affair seemed to have ended.

Bill paused to sip from his glass.

"You got all this from Monteath?" Jerry asked. "After last night?"

"In detail," Bill said. "Before that, it was an hypothesis — based on a nurse's memories.

A pattern into which things seemed to fit. It gave me an assumption — something to test out."

So — with Mrs. Monteath dead, with Parks dead, with Behren in the army, the Maine affair appeared to have come to an end. If Wilmot and his wife had not, while on vacation, happened to stop by the Monteath cottage, it probably would have ended there.

"And here, I'm still guessing," Bill said. "Wilmot's dead; Mrs. Wilmot doesn't know; Monteath says he doesn't know, whether Wilmot was involved in the blackmail attempt. I don't know. He may have been. He may not have been — the Wilmots' visit may have been entirely fortuitous. I rather suspect it was — and that Monteath's attitude, before the fact, aroused Wilmot's interest, after the fact. Monteath may have been obviously anxious to get rid of the Wilmots; Mrs. Wilmot thought he was. Wilmot may have suspected something was up. And if Wilmot was already involved in espionage, it would occur to him that Monteath might one day supply information, under pressure. The killing of Parks, if it wasn't what it seemed to be, would give the means of applying pressure. My guess would be that Wilmot kept an eye on things and, when Behren came into it, got in touch with Behren — and got information that, when the time came, he could use. Monteath wasn't ready for pressure then. He could be left to — well, to ripen, as he went on in the State Department. Wilmot could wait."

The precise pattern here was, Bill said again, a matter of hypothesis. Since other things fitted, the hypothesis was, clearly, correct in substance.

By the night of the April Fool's party, Monteath was, it appeared, considered ripe. He had information Wilmot could sell. So, Wilmot had arranged, in the elaborate disguise of a practical joke, a reminder for Monteath — a red-haired mannequin, enough like Behren, as Monteath had known Behren, to make the point; to remind Monteath of the past, and disclose that Wilmot knew of the past.

"It seems very elaborate," Dorian said, apparently to the cat named Sherry. "Oblique."

"A stratagem," Pam said, rounding it off.

Bill agreed. It would have been simpler for Wilmot to take Monteath aside and to whisper in his ear.

"But," Bill said, "the elaborate appealed to Mr. Wilmot. It always had. It was part of the design of his life."

There they had it — a fancy for devious progress toward goals: the surprised discomfiture of the butt of a jest; a highly dramatized warning to Arthur Monteath, through mimic repetition of murder. In both cases, the means as interesting to Wilmot as the end; in the latter case, a large and startled audience for a theatrical production. It was conceivable that Wilmot had regarded espionage itself, with its essential and necessary deviousness, as very like a practical joke.

In any event, Monteath had taken Wilmot's meaning. There had been a whispered conference then; Monteath had agreed to see Wilmot the next day, knowing that it was blackmail over again, but not this time for money.

"For what?" Jerry asked.

Bill Weigand hesitated. Then he shrugged, said he couldn't see that it mattered.

"A list of names," he said. "Names of people doing — well, they were described to me as doing 'little chores' for us in Eastern Europe."

"Spies," Pam North said.

Bill half smiled. He said she must know the United States government did not employ spies.

"Then the more fool it," Pam said. "Us."

"Anyway," Bill said, "Monteath had a little list. Not a written list. A list in his mind. He was taking it to Washington. Wilmot and company wanted it. Presumably, they planned to sell names from it to governments which might be interested."

"And get these people killed," Pam said. "Or put in prison for life or something."

She looked at it, Bill told her, as Monteath had. Monteath said Wilmot and Dewsnap were rats; he expressed no regret at having killed rats. He was sorry he had been caught.

"I'm not sure I'm not," Pam said. "Of course — "

They waited politely, but she did not finish.

Monteath had had no intention of parting with the list. On the other hand, he had no intention, if it could be avoided, of going on trial in Maine for murder. So he had stopped by the Norths' apartment after leaving the party, stayed long enough to make it reasonably certain that no lingering guest would remain in the penthouse and gone back up to pay an unexpected visit.

"But," Pam said, "we went to the elevator with him. And he went — " She stopped.

"Right," Bill said. "He said he was going down; you expected him to go down. It never occurred to you that he might as easily have gone up."

"But," Dorian said, "there's an indicator, or a light, or — "

"Stuck," Pam said. "It always thinks it's the fifth floor. Mr. Monteath had noticed that?"

"Right," Bill said. "He had."

He had gone up, but not to the door of the penthouse. He had gone up the fire stairs to the roof, over the low wall to the penthouse terrace and had found an open door leading to the kitchen.

"An open door?" Jerry said.

"Right," Bill said. "He'd opened it before he left. With the crowd there, there was no difficulty. He'd also noticed the knives."

So — in the kitchen he had waited, watched Wilmot finish a drink, picked up a knife, holding it so his arm hid it, walked in on a startled Wilmot and — used the knife.

"Then," Bill said, "he naturally threw the dummy off the roof."

They waited.

"Because it might be a link," Bill said. "It obviously was intended to resemble somebody. Monteath gave us credit, assumed we would notice this and investigate. We might identify the dummy with Behren, and Behren with Parks, and Parks with Monteath. By the time it hit the sidewalk twelve floors down, nobody was going to identify it with anybody. People would describe it, but — " Bill shrugged.

"I thought," Pam said, "that we described it very well. But I see what you mean."

Monteath had realized, of course, that the

descent of a man-sized dummy from a penthouse to the street below would be noticed, even late at night. He had taken care to drop it when nobody was passing; he had returned, sat down and waited. In due course, the police arrived below; subsequently, Sergeant Fox arrived at the door. Monteath impersonated Wilmot — a drunken Wilmot.

"The lowest common denominator," Pam said and Jerry, almost at the same time, said, "One drunk sounds like another." "I like my way better," Pam said. "Go on, Bill."

With Fox gone from the penthouse door, the police gone from the street, Monteath also went. He thought he had settled matters, and that he had made no revealing mistake.

"As a matter of fact," Bill said, "I don't know that he had — then."

But he had made a mistake, nevertheless. He had assumed Wilmot to be alone in the plot. He had thought Behren dead — Behren had been reported dead. He had never heard of Dewsnap. He heard from Dewsnap in a few hours; heard that Dewsnap knew what Wilmot had known; realized another rat remained alive.

"Two, counting Behren," Pam pointed out. Bill shook his head at that. Until after he was arrested, Monteath had not known that Behren, calling himself Albert Barron, was alive.

"And Frank?"

"A hired man, apparently," Bill said. "He's out of our hands, too. But I doubt whether he knew about Monteath, or that he had killed Wilmot. As a matter of fact, I'd guess that Frank thought Dewsnap had killed Wilmot or, perhaps, that Behren had. Almost certainly, it was Dewsnap who wrote the lines for the little play Frank acted out here yesterday afternoon."

Pam and Jerry North shook their heads. Dorian said that, for her part, she didn't understand any of it. She said it was the last time she was ever going to come in late.

"Sylvester Frank came here intending to be picked up," Bill said. "To tell the story involving Clyde Parsons — make us believe he had found Parsons's coat in the penthouse and that there was blood on it. He hadn't. He'd seen Parsons going toward this apartment house, all right, and without a coat. He'd told Dewsnap that, and that Parsons was pretty drunk. Dewsnap figured out the story."

"Why?" Pam said, and Jerry said, "Where was the coat?"

"As to the coat," Bill said, "I've no idea. Probably left it in some bar, and somebody picked it up. He seems to have thought he left it at his uncle's apartment, and Mrs. Wilmot said he left there without it. She lied to protect him — very fond of him, for some reason. The coat isn't there. Frank didn't take it away, as he says. Why should he? He was a hired hand. He hadn't been told what to do. His great fondness for Parsons — rats!"

"So many rats," Pam said. "Again — why, Bill? Why involve Parsons?"

"Part of the price Monteath was to get for the list," Bill said. "The Maine business would be forgotten. He would be got in the clear on Wilmot's murder. Dewsnap didn't go into details, Monteath says. Dewsnap was a man who played things close, apparently. He just told Monteath not to worry about killing Wilmot, that he'd see it was taken care of."

"And Mr. Monteath agreed?"

"Pretended to," Bill said. He finished his cocktail; he lighted a cigarette. He hesitated, and accepted another cocktail. "Actually, he was still rat hunting. He pretended he was willing to turn over the names. Promised to write them down. He said he would telephone Dewsnap when he was ready and that they would meet, where they wouldn't be seen. He did telephone Dewsnap last night, at Dewsnap's house in Brooklyn. They decided on the Emporium."

"Dewsnap was a fool," Jerry said.

"Well," Bill said. "Yes, as it turned out. He underestimated Monteath and overestimated himself. Dewsnap had been around a good bit, I gather. Figured he was up to any trick Monteath might think of. And Dewsnap had a gun in his desk drawer."

"And didn't use it?"

"No," Bill said. "You see — he was a little surprised during his last few seconds. He'd been expecting Monteath. He got — Mr. Punch. Quite startling and, of course, Dewsnap didn't know who it was for a moment. That was long enough. Monteath hit him on the head with a little metal statuette — very comical affair. We found it later. A monkey in a — well, an amusing posture. Meant to be amusing, anyway. Part of Wilmot's stock, of course. Then, to make sure, Monteath merely opened the office window and dropped Dewsnap on what remained of his head. He started to get away then. But — people started coming. Baker and some friends of his — a man named Saul, for one. Behren — he was the one who hit you, Jerry. Frank. Martha Evitts. To say nothing of you two. A gathering of the clan."

"Why Martha?" Pam asked. "She wasn't in the — clan?"

"No," Bill said. "They say not. Dewsnap called her at her apartment, she says. Told her — "

"I know," Pam said. "Why?"

293

Bill shrugged. They would never know precisely what had been in Dewsnap's mind. Bill could guess. He guessed that Dewsnap had identified Baker as "one of Saul's bright young men." He guessed that Dewsnap was about to wind things up; take flight. "Quite literally," Bill said. "To Mexico. He'd bought a ticket." Martha Evitts was to be used as a hostage, to buy time. But Dewsnap had already run out of time when Martha reached the Emporium.

"The money in Wilmot's safe?" Jerry asked.

When you were in the business of selling information, you often had to buy it.

"The fingerprints in the safe?"

"That was Baker's," Bill said. "He went over the place yesterday morning, when he found Wilmot dead. What he found in the safe, beside the money — well, I really don't know. Something, I'm pretty sure. But Saul and his boys — they're not often communicative." He finished his drink. "I," he said, "am very communicative."

"Parsons and Mrs. Wilmot?"

"Innocent bystanders," Bill said. "While everybody was chasing around in Wilmot's shop, they were at the movies."

There was a considerable silence, in the course of which Sherry snored suddenly, rather loudly.

"That reminds me — " Dorian began, but Pam said, "Wait!"

"I saw Mr. Baker hit a policeman," Pam said. "Very distinctly. Very hard, too."

"You don't give up," Jerry told her.

"No," Bill said. "She did, of course. Hit him quite hard. One reason Behren hadn't been as loquacious as they'd like, I gather. Jaw doesn't work too well."

"Mr. Behren?" Pam said. "A policeman?"

"No, Pam," Bill said. "Dressed as a policeman. As Monteath was dressed as Mr. Punch. And — Baker as a boy in rompers. Miss Evitts as a witch."

There was a longish pause.

"Well — " Dorian said, and lowered Sherry to the floor. Bill moved to get up. Incensed, Martini whirled, snarled, and lashed at Bill Weigand, with every evidence of jungle fury. She then leaped down, glared at the four of them, and left the room, indignation in each movement.

"As Pam says," Jerry noted, "you can always go by cats."

The employees of THORNDIKE PRESS hope you have enjoyed this Large Print book. All our Large Print titles are designed for easy reading, and all our books are made to last. Other Thorndike Large Print books are available at your library, through selected bookstores, or directly from us. For more information about current and upcoming titles, please call or mail your name and address to:

THORNDIKE PRESS
PO Box 159
Thorndike, Maine 04986
800/223-6121
207/948-2962